THE
RESTLESS
GIRLS

BLOOMSBURY CHILDREN'S BOOKS
Bloomsbury Publishing Inc., part of Bloomsbury Publishing Plc
1385 Broadway, New York, NY 10018

BLOOMSBURY and the Diana logo are trademarks of Bloomsbury Publishing Plc

First published in Great Britain in September 2018 by Bloomsbury Publishing Plc
Published in the United States of America in March 2019
by Bloomsbury Children's Books

Bloomsbury books may be purchased for business or promotional use. For information on bulk
purchases please contact Macmillan Corporate and Premium Sales Department at
specialmarkets@macmillan.com

Library of Congress Cataloging-in-Publication Data
available upon request
ISBN 978-1-5476-0072-4 (hardcover)
ISBN 978-1-5476-0073-1 (e-book) • ISBN 978-1-5476-0277-3 (e-PDF)

Printed and bound in China by C&C Offset Printing., Ltd.
2 4 6 8 10 9 7 5 3 1

All papers used by Bloomsbury Publishing Plc are natural, recyclable products
made from wood grown in well-managed forests. The manufacturing processes
conform to the environmental regulations of the country of origin.

To find out more about our authors and books visit www.bloomsbury.com and sign up for our newsletters.

JESSIE BURTON

THE
RESTLESS
GIRLS

ILLUSTRATED BY
ANGELA BARRETT

BLOOMSBURY
CHILDREN'S BOOKS
NEW YORK LONDON OXFORD NEW DELHI SYDNEY

For Florence Freeman,
with love

One

Princess Frida and the Mourning Curtain

Not far from where you're sitting right now, there exists a country called Kalia. It's a beautiful place, well worth visiting if you have the time. The capital is an ancient city named Lago Puera, and sailors and visitors usually enter through its port. They are greeted by the sight of the palace domes, sparkling in the sun, painted like the Kalian sea, whose waves foam silver, whose depths shade the eye with unending blues. The shore shimmers gold, the land opens like an emerald quilt, and the Kalian mountains rise up as giants to greet the sky.

You'd think that for the princesses in this story, who were

born in Kalia, who grew up in that palace, who were destined to survey the waters of the Kalian sea, this would be a happy place to live.

In fact, it was the opposite.

There were twelve of them, and the eldest was named Frida. Frida was very clever, and she had many ambitions, but most persistent was her desire to fly a plane.

Then came Polina, and she could read the stars.

Next was Lorna, the kindest, and thus the wisest, of them all.

After her was Ariosta, a talented painter, who cut off all her hair without permission when she was ten. (She had the same style ten years later: it still suited her.)

Chessa came next, a girl who sang to break your heart in twenty pieces, then put it back together with a jazzy aria.

Then came Bellina, who'd taught herself five languages.

Vita was the seventh daughter, a happy spirit, whose laugh was like a tonic. She was the luckiest, and the quickest at jokes.

Mariella came next, and she loved to do sums, numbers dancing in her mind like obedient bears.

Then there was Delilah, who had such a green thumb that even the stubbornest plant grew at her touch.

Next was Flora, always reading a book, a newspaper, or the side of a cookie box.

After her came Emelia, who wanted to be a vet.

And the youngest was Agnes, the most watchful of the sisters. She was going to be a writer when she grew up.

And their parents?

Well. This was the problem, as parents often are.

Queen Laurelia was their mother, dead before this story starts, but in her end is this beginning. Laurelia had been a woman of many words and the driver of a racing car—open top, leather seats, a craving for speed, and a fatal crash that was the bitterest unfairness her daughters ever tasted.

When they were very little, the princesses had never understood why it made their mother so happy to speed off down the road, goggles on, hair flying, metal gleaming, the engine roaring to a buzz and then to silence as she disappeared over the hill. Sometimes, at night, after Laurelia had died, Agnes thought she could feel the vibration of her mother's engine revving in her rib cage. Then she woke up and realized it was Emelia's snores. Agnes discovered that both the imagined and the real worlds could be equally comforting, and that sometimes it was very hard to tell the difference.

Never mind jewels and diadems, the words they'd heard from Laurelia were the princesses' inheritance: her songs down the corridors, her bedtime stories of other worlds. Her words roosted like birds in the girls' imaginations. In the days, weeks, and months after Laurelia's death, they took flight from her daughters' mouths and became their own.

Their father was named Alberto, and Alberto was king of Kalia. In the scheme of the story, this is a fact both important and irrelevant, like most things are, depending on the time of day you're looking at them. It was Alberto being king that made his daughters princesses. Now, between you and me, I don't think any of them liked being princesses very much. It might *seem* fun to wear a jeweled crown and have people do everything for you—but it quickly becomes tiresome, to the point that boiling an egg for yourself feels like a holiday.

After Queen Laurelia's death, King Alberto became the sort of person who ate a whole cake without offering anyone else a slice, and who punished his girls for things that weren't their fault at all. The girls weren't alone in this: the world is full of children picking up their parents' crumbs. Alberto and Laurelia had no sons, and I think this was part of the problem, because after Laurelia died, Alberto didn't know what to do with *one* daughter, let alone twelve of them. Laurelia had been the one watching them, nurturing their imaginations, their educations.

And now she was gone.

Growing up, Alberto had never learned a thing about girls; as a prince, all his friends were boys, and then as king, all his advisers were men. Girls in Kalia, whether they were princesses or not, had never been considered very important. Most important were the subjects of horse riding, hawking, killing small animals, sitting on thrones, and gathering taxes. When she was alive, Queen Laurelia had done her best to encourage her daughters to look forward to their adulthood, but it's hard when you're just one queen racing your motor against a long line of history trying to squash you down. No one had done such a thing for her when *she* was a little girl— they hadn't even thought it necessary to teach her how to read.

Every girl in Kalia was the same, and the people in charge of them clumped their individual hopes and dreams together like one big ball of moss. It didn't matter how well a girl could play the trumpet, or grow a sunflower, or write a poem, or solve a quadratic equation. *None* of that mattered. The best a girl could hope for was a marriage where the money was good and her husband didn't hog all of life's fun. A girl might as well have been a sunflower or a trumpet herself for all that her feelings were taken into consideration.

In the first week of mourning after Queen Laurelia's death, King Alberto dispensed with the girls' music lessons. He couldn't bear the sound of Chessa singing, he said, because she sounded too much like her mother. Chessa didn't open her mouth for days, not even to speak.

Then, in the second week of mourning, their mathematics tutor was dismissed, because princesses didn't need numbers. Mariella took to lying on her bed, tapping out times tables on her forearm.

By the third week of mourning, their botany classes were taken away from them. No longer were they allowed to take trips to the majestic Kalian mountains to collect plant samples for the palace laboratory. It wasn't just Delilah who had loved the clear air—all the girls enjoyed the mountains, where birds of extraordinary plumage called to one another from high trees, and the wildest flowers flourished.

Back at the palace, life was a tomb. The bright walls that Queen Laurelia had decorated were now shrouded in black velvet. No electric light was allowed; only candles were permitted—and their flames barely lit the corners of the huge, dark rooms.

The maids and cooks and butlers scurried along the walls, their shadows long and looming, heads down toward carpets that gathered dust because no one could see to clean them.

The sun, the gorgeous spanning sea beyond the windows, the sky such a blue, were shut out. Only melancholy was allowed to illuminate the girls' days.

The telephones—so recently installed, and such a thrill to Laurelia that she could speak to her sisters, who had married kings in other lands—were disconnected. The girls ached for that cheery metallic ring, which had always excited them, to know which far-off aunt was calling by the touch of her finger.

Now all was silence.

In the fourth week of mourning for the queen, King Alberto took away:

Ariosta's painting supplies,

all the girls' novels, poetry, dictionaries, encyclopedias, maps, comics, and newspapers,

Mariella's chemistry set,

Emelia's guide to looking after sick tigers,

Agnes's typewriter,

Polina's telescope,

Delilah's key to the greenhouse (the plants were left untended and began to die) . . .

and their mother's gramophone and all her jazz records.

Frida, who I told you was the cleverest, hid her airplane manuals in her underwear drawer. But regardless of this personal ingenuity, the girls were more miserable than they had ever been in their lives.

The king explained to the girls that they were now no longer allowed to go beyond the palace walls.

"But why?" asked Frida, surrounded as usual by the others. "You can't keep us locked in."

"I'm king, and I can," Alberto said. He sighed, scratching the top of his balding head through the circle of his crown. "I'm doing it because I love you," he went on. "I couldn't bear it if anything happened to you. It's so dangerous outside the palace walls."

"It's dangerous inside them too," Frida muttered as their father hurried off. He almost ran away from them, as if each of his daughters carried within her the spark of his dead wife, and their faces might pin him to the floor with grief.

By now, not even their eyes felt like the princesses' own, not even their hands and feet. Their hearts were gloomy; the palace guards watched them everywhere. Everything they saw and touched belonged to their father.

A yearning for their mother spread through the princesses' bodies like mold. It grew and grew, inside and over them, a creeping, seeping crust of pain swallowing them up—and the only things that might have kept them breathing, might have pushed back the mold a little bit, might have reminded them that they were still alive and deserved a chance to *enjoy* this fact, Alberto had taken away. The girls felt as dead as their mother.

Frida's sorrow over this turned to confusion, and finally to clarity and anger. She understood what that motor car had meant to Laurelia—it wasn't the car itself so much as what it had given her: a sense of movement, of direction. "You see, my darlings," Frida said to her younger sisters, "it made her feel *free*. And I'll tell you something else. The time for muttering is done."

Frida was true to her word, as she always was.

One fateful afternoon, after the princesses had endured yet another morning cooped up like twelve chickens with no promise of an egg, she stormed the corridors looking for their father. Polina and Lorna ran after her, trying to keep up. The other nine sisters scattered behind, a confusion of sad butterflies.

King Alberto was in the throne room as usual, the curtains closed. His advisers were standing in the shadows, unsure of what to do with their increasingly difficult monarch.

"Your Majesty," said Frida, coming toward him. "This isn't fair, and you know it. You cannot tell us how to grieve."

"Please go away," he said. "I can't bear to look at you."

"Father," Frida persisted. "We know you're sad, but we're sad too. Why take away our lessons, our music, our books, and our paints? They make us feel as if Mother is still here."

"Your mother is not here!" the king cried. "She's gone! Dead, by her own stupidity—and mine, for ever allowing her to drive that blasted racing car in the first place!"

"She loved that racing car," said Frida.

"Well, it didn't love her back," the king replied, screwing his face up like a horrible turnip. "I'm having it crushed."

"You can't!"

"Frida," said Alberto, "I'm the king. I can do what I want."

Frida pretended she hadn't heard. "Let me fix it with the help of the palace mechanic," she said.

"You'll do no such thing!" King Alberto snapped, losing his patience. "No man will marry a girl who fixes cars!"

"What does Mother's motor car have to do with getting married?" asked Frida.

(Frida, you may have noticed, never gave up.)

King Alberto's round cheeks turned tomato red, and he looked at his other eleven daughters, who had gathered behind Frida as she faced their father.

"Every one of you is a stick of dynamite!" he bellowed. "You'll explode me, and this kingdom—BOOM! Your mother was ridiculous about you, and now no one will touch you. Girls aren't supposed to do even a tiny *bit* of what you got up to. And look at what happened to her. Dead. *Dead!* I won't have it, I *won't!*" He slammed his hand on the arm of his throne, and his crown knocked slightly sideways.

"We're not sticks of dynamite," said Frida. "We're simply excellent girls."

King Alberto ignored her, throwing his hands up in the air. "Oh, why, why, *why* were we not blessed with a boy? Just one boy, one itty-bitty little boy, just one! That's all I ever asked for! I'm getting old, I feel a hundred—I look *two* hundred—and still no heir!"

"But you have twelve heirs," Frida said.

Alberto was used to these conversations with Frida. They'd been having them since she could talk, and he too would rarely give up. (In fact, I think that sometimes he rather enjoyed them.) "I have twelve girls," he said. "And what use are you? No woman can inherit my kingdom."

"Says who?" said Frida.

Alberto jumped from the throne as if his eldest daughter had slapped him in the face with a Kalian trout, and a large one at that. "It's the law!" he cried.

"Your Majesty," said Frida patiently. "*You* are the law."

His advisers shuffled on their feet like a group of perturbed pigeons. King Alberto was silent as he sat back into his throne, stroking his chin. For an agonizing, ecstatic moment, he actually seemed to be considering Frida's point. Agnes felt her heart lift, and the energy between her sisters' bodies shifted with hopeful anticipation. *Good old Frida,* she thought. *Quick as ever.*

14

But then their father stared down at them in horror, as if he was looking at his dead wife's image, a woman's lost face reflected in twelve young mirrors of fear. "None of you has the faintest idea what it takes to run a kingdom," he said.

Frida fell on her knees toward him, her arms open wide. "Because no one has ever taught us! But we'd learn. And have we not lived with your advisers our whole lives? I could lead a kingdom, I know I could. And if I couldn't, Polina could, and then there's—"

Alberto snorted. "*Polina?* Polina, who spends her life with one eye glued to a telescope?"

"But, Father," said Polina. "There is so much in the sky we've yet to learn—"

"No," interrupted Alberto, pointing at the floor. "Down *here* is what matters, not twinkling stars." He readjusted his crown.

"Father," said Frida, jumping to her feet and then pacing back and forth in front of the throne. "I want you to imagine something for me. Can you do that?" She looked at her father with a doubtful expression, as if it was unlikely he had any imagination left. "Imagine not being able to do anything, except *sit*."

"Sounds good to me."

"Except sit, and think about getting married. That's it, nothing else. Married to a man who doesn't even *exist* yet. And you can't even sit at a window with a view, because they're all covered over with black cloth."

"It'll do you good to calm down," he said. "Respect your mother's memory."

"We will respect her by carrying on as we did when she was alive."

"Your Majesty," Agnes piped up, encouraged by her sister's fire, "imagine . . . imagine that our hearts are lions, needing to jump and play, and feed and drink, and grow."

Frida laughed with joy. "Oh yes, Agnes!" she said. "Our hearts are lions!"

"Your hearts are *what?*" spluttered Alberto. "You're not lions! You and your ridiculous ideas, Agnes. Grow up."

He turned from his youngest daughter back to his eldest. "Frida. Be an example to the others, *please*. Think of your marriages, and accept that no girl, no woman, could ever be smart enough for my job."

Frida narrowed her eyes. "You wish me to be an example to the others?" she said.

16

Alberto folded his arms and stared at his defiant daughter. "Frida, it's my dearest wish."

"Very well, Your Majesty," she said.

The king sighed with relief, but everyone else in the room knew Princess Frida better. There was a beat. The room was silent, waiting to see what she would do next.

Frida walked, head held high, toward the curtain covering one of the windows.

When they realized what she was about to do, the advisers cried in unison for her to stop.

But Frida did not stop.

With one sharp heave, she pulled the curtain back, and a golden vengeance poured into the room.

"Insolence!" screamed the king, and in that moment it was hard to tell whether he was blinded by the light of the sun or his daughter.

Frida was moving like a spirit, curtain to curtain, pulling down the black drapes, advisers and maids cringing with their eyes closed, the dust swirling like gold motes around the throne as velvet and taffeta tumbled to the floor. Ariosta rushed to help her,

and Bellina followed, then Chessa and Delilah and Mariella, then Polina and Emelia, then Flora and Vita, and finally Lorna and Agnes, twelve princessly pairs of hands making portal after portal of sunshine to flood the room.

No one could stop them,

no one dared go near them,

and thus their father's throne was nothing,

a chair bleached white by the light of grief.

Two

King Alberto's Bad Decision

I don't think it's exactly right to say Frida *regretted* her performance in the throne room—for who could ever regret a slice of sunshine?—but the consequences for her and her eleven sisters were dire. As I've mentioned: it was a fateful afternoon.

True, Alberto didn't crush Laurelia's racing car to pieces, despite his threats. He had it renovated and sealed up inside the palace garage, where it started to gather dust, and a family of mice took up residence in the passenger seat.

But just when the girls thought life couldn't get any worse, it got worse.

Three days after the curtain incident, King Alberto, flanked by his advisers, summoned his daughters to a room in the palace they'd never seen before.

"You'll be perfectly safe in here," he said.

By now, the girls had barely enough energy to lift their heads and peer in, but when they did, they stared in horror at their new surroundings.

It was a room with no windows.

It contained twelve beds, in two facing rows of six. Off to the side was one small bathroom. On the far wall, hanging between the ends of the rows of beds, was a truly enormous portrait of Queen Laurelia in her motor-racing gear, as if to remind the girls what might happen if they ever tried to go faster than was appropriate.

"Good *lord*," said Ariosta, staring up at the painting. The other girls could barely look at it.

"You can't do this to us," said Frida, turning to her father and the advisers, several of whom were looking puffed up and pleased with themselves. "We used to play in Lago Puera and the mountains beyond. We used to make chemistry experiments in the royal laboratory. We used to play music in our own little band! Now this is what you do to us?"

"It's for your own good," replied the king. His expression was horribly blank, which was worse than him being angry.

"No," said Frida. "We were destined to survey the waters of the Kalian sea. *Everyone* told us that. You always said it yourself."

"I did. But in happier days."

"We deserve happier days again. Instead, you would put us in a cell, where we cannot even hear the waves? You would

23

shrink our lives to this small room, and a frozen picture of our mother's face—"

"Frida, stop!" said Alberto. "One of these days you will go too far."

"No," she replied. "I fear I won't go far enough." She took up Agnes's hand, which had begun to tremble.

"You can't be serious about this, Father," said Polina, attempting reason, wishing to thaw the air of hostility.

"I'm most serious," he replied. "One hour a day out in the palace grounds to stretch your legs."

Frida still hadn't given up. She turned to the king's advisers. "Gentlemen. Surely, for the good of Kalia, we should have our telescopes and typewriters back. Surely, instead of worrying about whether your princesses are going to explode, you should be concerning yourselves with your harvests, and your relations with the borderlands?" There was a slight panic in her voice now, and it scared the other princesses. They huddled behind her, hugging one another tight.

The advisers looked away, but Frida was right. (Frida was often right when it came to matters of state, although no one ever listened to her.) The kingdom of Kalia was falling apart, but Alberto was more obsessed with keeping his daughters locked safely away than doing his kingly duty.

None of the advisers wanted to lose his job, so they said nothing. Frida turned up her chin in disgust. "Cowards," she said. One of them, at least—her father's youngest adviser, a whippety-thin man called Clarence—looked shamefaced.

"You've all gone crazy," said Ariosta.

"Not crazy, just sensible," said the king. He brandished a heavy iron key at Frida. "Inside," he said. "*Now*. And please," he pleaded, "just go to sleep."

The advisers ushered them in, and each princess found a bed. They heard the key turn in the lock, a horrid grating sound that plunged their hearts into their feet.

There was no natural light, no privacy, no place for them to hide away with their thoughts. All Agnes wanted to hear was Emelia's little snores, to remind her that once they'd had a mother who loved a motor's engine. But instead the room hummed with the nervous energy of twelve young minds, crawling up the walls with no way out.

That day, the princesses learned that the line between crazy and sensible is a very fine line indeed.

⁕

It went on like this for weeks. The girls were kept in the room, allowed one hour a day for a walk, and their mother's painted face greeted them on their return. The maids brought their meals to the door, and the girls ate on their beds. King Alberto had ordered that they should be given a plain diet of porridge and toast, morning and night, with the occasional orange, but the girls barely noticed what was passing their lips.

They slept very badly. Frida said it felt as if they were getting older as their mother stayed young. And, of course, the painting's expression did indeed stay the same, friendly but distant, Queen Laurelia's mouth slightly open on a word they would never hear. "Oh, if only she would walk out of the frame and take us to the mountain!" Frida cried, tossing the skin of yet another orange to the floor.

It was such a sad sight, these wilting girls, that I can hardly bear to type it. But I've since learned that sadness comes and goes, and typewriters win out.

You see, the king could control the paths his daughters trod; he could take away their pleasures and their views and lock them up. He could make sure that the princesses didn't have anything in that room except their toothbrushes and tiaras, pajamas and nightgowns. But king or no king, there was one thing they possessed that he could never own: their imaginations.

Have *you* ever tried getting into someone else's imagination? It's practically impossible. Our inability to do so has caused headache and heartache since time began. Even your own imagination can be a slippery thing—you can't see it, you can't hold it, but you can certainly *feel* it. It can fill your day with sunshine or with storm. It will conjure worlds from nowhere and make them real. It will open doors you didn't even know existed; it will show you secrets that are yours alone. And the strange thing about imagination is that it can fly absolutely anywhere, even when your body stays in one place. I've seen it happen.

Imagination was the greatest weapon those girls had.

And one night, sitting up in their beds, telling stories as they always did, the princesses did indeed discover a secret.

It was the most perfect, timely secret, like moonlight on a pillow in a windowless room. It changed their lives forever.

And what was the secret?

Oh, go on then. Seeing as it's you.

Three

The Secret

That night—that particular night when everything changed—
it was Frida's turn to tell a story. The others had climbed out
of their own beds and were gathered on hers—quite a squeeze,
as you might imagine. They always liked it when it was Frida's
turn because, as the eldest, she had the most memories of Queen
Laurelia. But sometimes Frida told stories that were only half a
memory, and the other half was made up—"Because really," she
would say, "who can tell the difference?"

The lamps were lit as usual—twelve glowing orbs around the
room. The princesses felt as if they were living in a jewel box, their
hair and silk pajamas golden in the light.

Frida was just about to start her story, when she lifted her lamp toward the portrait of their mother. "Has someone moved the painting?" she asked. "It's *crooked*."

The other princesses looked over at the painting. It was true: Queen Laurelia was looking back at her daughters at a slight angle.

"I haven't touched it," said Flora.

"She never said you did, dearest," said Delilah.

"Maybe Vita knocked it by mistake," said Chessa. "There's barely room to breathe in here."

"Tell us a story, Frida. *Please*," said Lorna, sensing that everyone was a bit crotchety.

But Frida had slipped off the bed and was standing close to her mother's painting. "I'll tell you a story in a minute," she said. "But don't you think her eyes are inviting us in?"

"Inviting us in where?" asked Polina.

Frida touched the edge of the frame in an attempt to straighten it, and her hand froze. "*No*," she said. "That's *impossible*."

"What? What is it, Frida?" whispered Agnes as her skin turned to goose bumps.

Frida turned to her sisters, her face pale. "Can you come and help me lift the painting off?" she said. The sisters rushed over and did as they were asked, staggering with the weight of their mother's portrait. All twelve of them shuffled between the beds with the frame, propping Queen Laurelia to one side.

Frida held up her lamp to the wall. "By all the stars of Kalia," she breathed. "I wondered, but I hardly dared hope."

In the flickering light of her lamp, the others could see what Frida had thought was impossible, but which, in fact, was true.

"Is that . . . a *door*?" whispered Emelia.

Emelia was quite right. It was a thin outline of a door, a panel embedded in the wall. Frida reached out. Her hand could touch it, feel it! It was *real*.

"How did we never notice this before?" she asked her sisters, but none of them could answer.

The door was made of the same material as the wall, and there was no handle. Frida pushed the panel, and under her touch it swung back easily. The other girls joined her and stood around the threshold. All they could see was pitch black, as if they were standing on the edge of a deep pit. Cold air hit their cheeks and knocked the breath out of them. In the silence, from somewhere deep and far away, Agnes thought she could hear music, the sweet jazzy waft of a clarinet. A strange smell she'd never tasted before rose up: heady, heavy, a little smoky, like a raspberry dipped in black amber. A tinkling of bells, the lap of a wave. It was most unsettling.

And most exciting.

For a moment, no one said anything. It felt as if they were teetering between an old life and a new.

"Where does this lead?" asked Mariella.

"Good question. Who knows? But I'm going to find out," replied Frida.

"I'm coming with you," said Vita.

"Me too," said Ariosta.

"We'll *all* go," said Frida. "No one should be left behind."

"But it could be dangerous," Bellina cried, leaping to Frida's side and hanging on her sleeve. "It might be a trap."

"A trap?" said Frida, laughing. "I think we've been trapped long enough, don't you?"

"I don't want something bad to happen. What would Father say—?"

"He's not going to say anything, my sweet, because we're not going to tell him," said Frida. "And, Bellina, *think*. What could be worse than being holed up here for another night?"

Bellina bit her lip.

"Darling Bell," said Lorna. "What Frida's saying is true. And if I have to spend one more evening in this tiny room with nothing to do except count sheep and polish my tiara, I might go crazy."

"I'm surprised I'm not crazy already," said Emelia. "We have to go."

"Well said, both of you," said Frida. "This door is exactly what we need. Hurry!" she went on, shooing her sisters. "Dressing gowns and shoes. Fetch your lamps. Voices down. Father's guards may be on the other side of the walls, wherever it is we're going."

The princesses found their lamps, put on their shoes, and followed their eldest sister to the edge of the strange door.

Frida held her lamp over the threshold, and the light opened up the darkness like a dancer cast from orange flame, jumping and jutting, finding its way. The others waited with bated breath for her to tell them what she could see.

"A staircase!" she whispered. "Oh, it goes down and down and down! I can't imagine how many steps there are. It's so *dark*."

Nevertheless, one by one, the princesses began to follow her

down,

    and down,

        and down,

           and down,

                their lamps held high,

            their soles echoing

        and echoing

on the stone steps.

The staircase did not appear to have been used for years. Cobwebs clung to their faces and stuck to their hair. There was a new smell of mold and damp, and the air was still horribly cold.

"Do you think Mother went down this staircase?" asked Mariella. "Did she ever mention one to you, Frida?"

Frida was silent for a moment. "Do you know, Mari, I think she might have. But only when I was tiny."

"I don't like it," Polina whispered over Frida's shoulder. "We're going underground. What if there are spiders?"

"The stars will be waiting for you when we come back, Pol. And as for spiders, they'll be more frightened of you. Keep

36

walking," Frida whispered back. "I'm sure this is something important."

After about fifteen minutes, the girls, dizzy from the continual spiraling downward and the fluff of cobweb in their eyes, finally reached a flat level. They held up their lamps again. They could see nothing beyond them but darkness. All they could hear was their own blood beating in their bodies, and their breath on the cool air.

"That was five hundred and three steps," whispered Mariella. "I counted."

"I think we're deep beneath the palace," said Flora. She held her lamp higher. "And look—there's the mouth of the sea!"

But it was not the mouth of the sea. Beyond was a lagoon—a wide, deep, dark underground pool—lit around its edges and in the crannies of its rocks by tiny lights that blinked from the darkness like stars.

When Polina looked at it, she wondered why she'd ever been worried. It felt as if they'd traveled upward into a firmament of celestial wonder, not deep beneath the surface of their father's land. It was a breathtaking vision.

Agnes ran to the lagoon's edge.

"Don't touch it!" said Flora, for she had read many stories of tempting and beautiful sights that would only lead a princess to her doom.

"I'm not going to touch it," said Agnes. "I'm just trying to work out how we're going to cross it."

The others joined her and stared at the water. It was as deep as a dream from which you might never wake. They shivered; for all its beauty, they felt that perhaps they shouldn't hang around. And then came the noise of the music again, that sweet melodious sound of a single clarinet, from somewhere across the lagoon, and it felt to the girls as if it was calling them to join it.

"Maybe we should swim across?" said Ariosta, beginning to roll up her pajama legs. "It's been ages since I had a dip."

"I—Ari—really?" said Bellina.

"Let her," said Frida. "Ariosta's the best swimmer out of all of us, and sometimes a dolphin just has to swim."

"But what if there's something in the water?" whispered Flora.

"There's always something in the water," said Ariosta, grinning, and she sat by the side of the lagoon and plunged in one leg and then the other. The girls held their breath, but nothing bad happened to

their sister. Ariosta splashed her legs around, the drops illuminated by the twinkling lights. "Oooh! It's *freezing*!" she said, which made them laugh for the first time since their mother died.

Emboldened by her intrepid sister, Bellina dipped her hand into the water. "It feels like Mother's shirts," she said. "So satiny!"

"Don't drink it," warned Lorna. "It's bad enough that one of us is swimming in it."

"I don't want to drink it; I just want to swim in it. I'll be back," said Ariosta.

"It'll be all right, Lorn," said Frida. "Trust me."

"Oh, Ari," said Delilah proudly. "You really are a fantastic fish."

They waited in silence, holding their lamps up as high as they could to illuminate Ariosta's swim. The minutes ticked.

"I've found something!" Ariosta called, and her sisters breathed a sigh of relief.

"What is it?" Polina shouted back. "Ari, be careful!"

"Hold on—it's so dark," Ariosta replied. And then—"Oh! I've found . . . some boats!"

The sisters cheered and clapped as Ariosta swam back and forth six times, bringing six boats to their side of the lagoon, six boats that turned out to fit two princesses apiece. When Ariosta was finished and had pulled herself out of the water, her sisters hugged her so tightly, and covered her with so many of their dressing gowns until her teeth stopped chattering, that she looked happier than she had in over a year.

Two by two, the girls lowered themselves into the bobbing

vessels and set off across the water. Chessa splashed her oars into the dark, her eyes on the bank ahead. She hummed a quiet tune, gently testing the acoustics of the rocks above.

The others, who loved to hear her sing and who had missed it terribly since King Alberto had stopped their music lessons, kept their own oars as quiet as they could, hoping they might hear again the glorious sound of their childhood.

They were in luck. After what had felt to them a lifetime, Chessa took a deep breath, closed her eyes, opened her mouth, and began to sing:

"The girls rowed on a dark lagoon
In the cave's imaginary night.
They didn't know why
But still in the sky—
There burned a beautiful light!"

Chessa's voice reverberated across the water and around the rocks in a magical echo. "Oh, Chess," Frida called from the boat she was sharing with Agnes. "You always pop my heart like a champagne

42

cork." The others laughed at the truth of Frida's words, for Chessa's singing did fizz their blood like the finest bubbles. Then far off came the clarinet again, as if it was replying to the power of Chessa's voice, waiting impatiently for her to give it more music.

"Mother used to sing that to me at bath time," said Chessa after she stopped, now dipping her fingers in the lagoon.

"Well, Mother was right," said Flora. *"Look!"*

The girls turned toward the bank. It was as if the words of Chessa's song had conjured the sight before them. Where minutes before all had been darkness, now, through a crack in the rock beyond, narrow enough for one princess at a time, there was indeed a light.

This light sparkled more than any knife or fork the girls had used at their parents' banquets. This light seemed to burn brighter than the moon, as its shining rays beckoned them in. This light was extraordinary.

"What *is* it?" said Emelia as the girls jumped out of the boats and tied them to various rocks lining the new side of the lagoon.

"We won't know until we go a little closer," said Agnes. "Frida, wise to pursue?"

All the sisters turned to Frida. Frida looked first at the moored boats, secondly at Agnes's hopeful little face, and then toward the lagoon, darker than a thought that never ends.

"It would be a shame," she said, "given how enterprising Ariosta has been with getting us over the water, and how observant Chessa has been about this light, *not* to carry on. To do anything else feels wrong. Agnes, you shall lead the way."

Agnes's small body puffed up with pride and pleasure at such responsibility, and the older sisters hid their affectionate smiles at their little walking popcorn. With Agnes at the fore, princess after princess slipped through the crack in the rock. Once they were all safely through, they abandoned their lamps and approached the glowing magnificence.

Any fear they might have been holding in their hearts was forgotten. The light made their cheeks pale, their eyes shining coins, their hair a moving field of silver wheat. As they kept on, the princesses soon realized they were walking through the most beautiful forest. They trod a delicate path lined by tall and slender birch trees, each leaf on the branches a glorious, shimmering pocket of light. Silver birds sang to one another, glimpsed through the foliage like falling stars.

"I can't believe it," whispered Polina. "I'm sure I dreamed of such a place when I was a little girl!"

"Me too," said Frida, turning up her face in wonder.

"Me three," breathed Lorna.

The eldest three sisters agreed that the silver forest, for all its surprise, also had the air of familiarity—as if, once upon a time, someone had told them about it, as if it had always been there, waiting for them to return. Frida scrunched up her face, trying to remember where, how, *why* this place felt like a second home. But it was no use—and Frida knew when it was best to accept a mystery and not pull its wings off, like a brute might to a butterfly.

After a while, the birches started to thin out, and the calls of the silver birds fell silent. The light that had cloaked them faded away, and everything went dark. Polina looked up, in case there were any stars she could use to guide their way—but she couldn't see a thing. The girls stopped walking and formed a circle, holding hands, palm against damp palm as they looked outward on the endless night.

"I wish we still had our lamps," whispered Bellina.

"What do we do now?" asked Delilah.

"We could retrace our steps," Mariella suggested.

"We don't know where those steps *are*, it's so dark," replied Vita.

It was true. They'd lost their bearings. They were surrounded by a nothingness, a looming absence of landscape and dimension, depth and time. A strange feeling of uncertainty crept up the backs of their legs and spines, into their stomachs, their throats, their eyes. It was as if the silver forest, the lagoon, the staircase—even the palace upstairs—had never existed.

Without warning, Emelia broke the circle and dropped down onto all fours. "Shh!" she said. "Can you hear that?"

"Hear what?" said Flora.

"*That*," replied Emelia. "Where are you?" she called. "I can hear you!"

"Who is she talking to? Has she gone crazy?" said Vita.

But then the other sisters began to hear it too, a faint sound of dried leaves swishing, a thrum of movement on the air.

"Maybe it's one of Father's advisers, come to punish us," said Ariosta. The girls huddled closer together against this new fear.

"Never," said Frida. "They're not brave enough to come down here."

Emelia kept on crawling around in the dark and called gently, "Don't be scared. I'll help you."

As she said this, a small fox crawled into view.

Now, you probably know what a fox looks like.

Perhaps you picture a proud red coat, neat and springy black legs, intelligent eyes the color of an orange stone?

Well, this fox didn't look like that. *This* fox had green eyes and fur like tarnished gold, a weak star fallen in the girls' circle. He was dragging one of his back legs. It was broken, and little whimpers were coming from his damaged body. Suddenly, the girls forgot their own worry and turned instead to this beautiful, suffering creature, so fantastical he could have climbed out of a treasure chest.

Emelia got to her feet and went over to Mariella. Without warning, she dug deep in her sister's dressing-gown pocket. "Aha!" she said, pulling out Mariella's favorite wooden ruler. "I *knew* you still had it. Perfect for a splint."

"Hold on—"

But Emelia was down again, facing the fox. She put out a hand,

and he turned his muzzle, sniffing the scent of her welcome on the air. He approached her—slowly, timidly—his emerald eyes fixed on her in the hope that she would remove his pain.

"But that's my best ruler!" said Mariella.

"We'll make sure you have a new one, sweetheart," Frida replied. "By the looks of it, right now that little creature needs it more than you."

Emelia whipped off her dressing-gown cord and fashioned it into a bandage against the fox's leg. The fox didn't flinch under her ministrations. He kept quite still, as if he trusted her. The other eleven girls admired their sister, her deftness, her confidence, her gentle handling of such a frightened being.

Emelia finished securing the fox's bad leg into a splint.

"I'm sure it's glowing brighter," said Agnes, and it did seem as if the fox had absorbed Emelia's expertise. His golden fur was shining; his body beamed like a living lantern. Nudging Emelia's hand as if to say *thank you*, he trotted out of the circle, three good legs padding on the ground, his healing leg treading lighter. The girls followed the fox's glow, happy that Emelia's skill had led them from that place of doubt.

As they followed the fox, the princesses noticed that the air had warmed, its texture thicker. A forest of oaks began to appear, trees with bark so shining the sisters were dazzled by their light. Delilah patted one of the trunks. "These must be made of gold!" she said. When the others touched it too, it certainly felt to them like something precious.

The forest where the fox had led them became a glowing goblet. In the canopy that beamed above, every leaf on every tree turned honey, amber, topaz, ruby. It was as if the world was on fire, and they were standing in the center of their father's crown. Delighted, they spun around and around until the forest was nothing but a bright blur.

But by the time they steadied themselves, the little fox had vanished.

"We must keep walking," said Frida. "This adventure isn't over yet." She looked around at her sisters. Their eyes were bright; they were chatting among themselves. "We have to keep going."

"Can't we just stay here?" said Flora. "It's so beautiful."

"We could. But I think something even more special is waiting for us at the end," said Frida.

And as she uttered these words, just as the forest of silver had done, the forest of gold began to disappear. The darkness grew around them once more. But this time the princesses were not frightened. They knew now that the dark was simply the beginning of new things. The dark was necessary. The dark might bring you a golden fox. The dark could be kind to twelve girls simply looking for their next path.

And soon enough, they could hear the tinkling of bells, the same they had heard while standing in their bedroom at the top of the staircase.

As they kept on through the dark, following this sound, a forest of diamonds appeared, diamonds hanging everywhere in heavy vines of brilliance, a splendor that outshone even the forests of silver and gold. Nature itself was a jewel. Beholding this sight, the girls felt themselves to be as powerful as the glittering stones draping every inch of the underground world they had discovered.

Delilah approached the shining vines, her eyes wide in wonder. "It can't be!" she whispered. She stood before the sinewy, silvery ropes, not daring to touch them.

"What is it, Delly?" Chessa asked.

"It's a dormidon plant," said Delilah. "The diamonds are growing on its vines."

"My goodness!" said Bellina.

"I'd read that they existed," Delilah went on, the excitement growing in her voice, "but no one's ever seen one in the flesh. It's such a powerful plant, and that's why diamonds choose to grow on it."

"How beautiful it is!" said Agnes.

As the other girls ran over to join Delilah and Agnes, to take in the twisting, twinkling, intoxicating strings of stones, they realized the source of those tinkling bells: it was the diamonds themselves, moving against one another on the vines.

"The seeds live inside the vine," Delilah said. She turned to her eldest sister. "Do you . . . do you think I could take some back with me, Frida? Just to see if I could grow one in the palace gardens, if Father ever lets me?"

Frida put her hands on her hips and stood back to survey the thick, swaying curtain of dormidon vines. From somewhere very near came the sound of that clarinet, except now there was something else—a beating drum—and was that a trumpet, so fast and lively and exciting? The other sisters looked at one another: they could hear it too.

"I promise you, Delilah," Frida said, "that one day you will return to those gardens. So you'd better take some dormidon with you, for when the moment comes."

Delilah stepped in among the vines and gently tugged one. It came away in her hands like a girl's cut braid. She tucked it into her dressing gown pocket and began to wander farther in.

"Let me help you, Delly," said Frida, reaching toward the cool plant, feeling the icy touch of the diamonds as they tumbled from the vine onto the forest floor. "You're going to need a bit more."

"How can you possibly know that?" asked Mariella.

Frida shrugged. "Just a feeling. Sometimes a feeling can be as true as fact."

Mariella laughed at this, but she helped her sisters with the vines regardless. Bellina joined in too, and then all the princesses, and as several hands touched the swaying ropes, something astonishing happened.

With a *whoosh*, a whole sheet of vines and diamonds fell to the forest floor, revealing the most incredible sight any of the princesses had ever seen.

None of them could speak. They simply stood there in their dressing gowns. All they could do was stare at the scene beyond them, as the dormidon vines snaked silvery around their feet.

And what did they see? It's not easy to describe. But seeing as you've come this far with me, I will most definitely try.

It was a gigantic tree, probably the biggest tree they'd ever seen, and bigger even than that. At the front of this gigantic tree, the twists of its own roots—the thickest, strongest, highest roots imaginable—made an arch wide enough, and tall enough, for a three-story house to fit beneath with room to spare.

"I can see lights in there!" said Agnes.

"And can you hear that wonderful music?" said Chessa.

They looked closer: under that soaring arch of roots, deep in its heart, a hollowed entrance hall spanned out in shining tiles of black and white. Around the hall, lights of every color bobbed like fireflies, while above, hanging from the ceiling, clear chandeliers glittered like illuminated raindrops.

It felt wonderful to be near. In a funny way, it was just as they

imagined it would be, even though they didn't know they were coming and they'd never seen it before. It felt like in this place the girls might have nothing to worry about, nothing to fear.

"Wise to pursue?" Agnes whispered to her eldest sister.

"Wise to pursue," replied Frida, and Agnes was sure that Frida had quickly wiped away a tear.

Four

A Dance and a Doughnut

The girls moved as if in a living dream. Never in their lives had they desired something as much as they desired to enter that tree.

But *just* as they had walked under the soaring tree roots and were about to set foot on that black-and-white floor, they heard a voice.

A blustering, slightly squeaky, indignant voice.

"Do you have the right to come in here?" asked the voice. "Oh, goodness me. There's *twelve* of you?"

They looked down. To their surprise, a peacock had appeared

before them, his tail feathers spread. He wore a red velvet waistcoat that could not meet across the plump brilliance of his turquoise chest. His wings clutched a huge leather book, gold letters across it spelling out the words: *Necessary Guests*. The feathers on the crown of his head quivered in a way that was strangely familiar to the twelve sisters.

"I beg your pardon?" said Lorna, who could not abide rudeness.

"You can't just *walk* in here, you know," said the peacock. "You have to *be expected*."

"Saleem," said another voice. "Please calm down."

From across the black-and-white floor came a lioness. Her voice was very different: smooth and deep, a little smoky, warm as a rug on a cold winter night. She was big, and the girls shrank away a little in fear. Her fur shone under the multicolored lights, changing rainbow shades as she strode toward them. Her paws were huge, the size of dinner plates, and her eyes burned with an intelligence that intimidated the girls.

The lioness sat up straight before them. "Page thirty-five, Saleem," she said patiently.

Saleem riffled through the pages of his book, even as his

own feathers ruffled with indignation. "Ah!" he squeaked. "The *princesses*. I see. Yes, yes." He cleared his throat. "Item: found door to staircase, and descended despite spiders. Item: sourced boats and crossed lagoon. Item: walked the three forests, and endured doubt. Item: befriended, tended, and mended the fox. Item: identified the dormidon among the diamonds. Item: discovered the tree palace."

The lioness examined her claws. "Brave, resourceful, clever, and kind. And terribly imaginative. Just how I like princesses to be." She grinned, retracting the claws. The girls still felt a little unsure. The lioness extended her front right paw. "I wasn't sure you were ever going to find us,' she said. 'But I'm glad you did."

Frida was the first to shake the lioness's paw. "Perhaps you've been expecting us," she said. "I believe we have a reservation."

Lioness and princess eyed each other, and each seemed satisfied by what they could see. "You have indeed," replied the lioness. She swished her majestic tail. "Welcome to the tree palace."

"The what?" said Agnes, forgetting her manners in a moment of curiosity.

"The tree palace. You're a little late, but Saleem and I appreciate that sometimes one's delays are not one's fault," the lioness went on. "Moreover, of course, certain guests never know they're coming to the tree palace until they find it."

"Very true," said Saleem. "I call it the reverse search." He peered at the girls. "Often happens with the likes of you. Down here, you don't find what you're looking for, but you will find what you need."

One by one, the other girls lined up to shake the lioness's paw. And a strange thing happened when human palm met feline pad: each of the princesses felt a touch of power. It was as if they had drunk a mug of hot chocolate and it was coursing through their bodies, with a little kick of chili at the end. It felt, quite frankly, *marvelous*.

"We could hear music," said Chessa.

"Ah, *that's* how you did it. Of course!" said the lioness. "Well, I expected you girls to have excellent taste. I do love jazz." She swept a paw back to welcome the girls in.

"My goodness," said Emelia. "Can you smell the food?"

The princesses were starving; they hadn't eaten a morsel since the cook's thin porridge many hours ago. And indeed, on the air, there was a mixture of the most delicious cooking aromas the girls had ever smelled.

"I can smell lamb chops," said Lorna.

"Juicy ones!" said Vita.

"Sprigged with rosemary," said Flora.

"*Look*," said Polina, and she pointed to a trestle table at the back of the dance floor.

On this trestle table there were indeed lamb chops, and next to these the princesses could also see doughnut pyramids— and next to *these*, glistening berry tarts and roast chickens. Oh, how they wanted to touch the tiny caraway-seed rolls and curls of the creamiest butter! There were peppercorn biscuits piled high like a pastry chef's countinghouse. Fountains of elderflower fizz frothing in the finest glasses they'd ever seen.

They wanted to dip their fingers into the tureens of bubbling chocolate sauce and the ice creams to pour it on, flavors of cinnamon, orange, vanilla, and coconut all mingling in the air. They wanted it all.

Around the edges of the dance floor, small circular tables had been arranged, with tasseled, pristine tablecloths. And in the near distance, a band of musicians was playing jazz—the jazz they'd been hearing so far away, for so long—now here, before them, sweet and clear, free and joyous! The girls felt a happiness they had never dared hope could be theirs again.

The lioness gazed at their pajamas and dressing gowns. "I *adore* your evening attire. A little louche, yes, but inimitably stylish."

"Hold on," said Mariella. "Are they . . . bears?"

"Oh yes," replied the lioness. "Dancing bears."

Two bears were shimmying in sequin skirts while a leopard played the clarinet. A tiger was playing the piano, a monkey was on the sax, a tabby cat was on the trumpet, an ostrich in a red beret was shaking her tail feathers, and three tortoises were working together, one on top of the other, to strum the double bass.

The music they were making was perfect to the girls' ears: lively, happy, and quick. It was dizzying to watch them.

"I'm *starving*," said Ariosta, her eye on the teetering trestle table.

"Then you shall eat," said the lioness. "You've done so well to get here, it's the least we can do." She grinned indulgently. "We're a bit off the beaten track. So take your table, and the waiters will be with you."

The girls did as she said, and the lioness clicked her claws. A toucan flew over, depositing a perfect jelly doughnut on Ariosta's plate. In fact, all the waiters were toucans, flying from girl to girl with menus in their beaks.

"Try that doughnut for starters," said the lioness. "Then take your fill."

Ariosta took a bite and

rolled her eyes in amazement. *"Unf.* This is the best jelly doughnut I've ever tasted."

The girls ordered from the toucan waiters, who obligingly flew hither and thither, fetching lamb chops and chicken legs, squishy cheeses and hot buttered toast, sausage and mashed potatoes, glasses of elderflower fizz, strawberries dipped in chocolate, and cups of smoky black tea that seemed to contain within it all the spices of the world.

"How do you like the place so far?" the lioness asked Frida.

Frida sat back in her chair, holding a glass of elderflower fizz as she surveyed the inside of the tree palace: the dance floor, the glittering chandelier, her sisters' delighted, happy faces at the food and music surrounding them. "It's funny," she said, "but it's just like the forests of silver, gold, and diamonds."

"What do you mean?"

"I mean that this tree palace seems to have been waiting for us particularly."

The lioness nodded. "Tree palaces are a bit like that."

"It feels like home," said Frida.

The lioness shook her large head, her whiskers glinting in

the lights. "Oh, no. The tree palace isn't your home. You mustn't think it is."

"But it's so much nicer than what we've got upstairs!"

"Well. It *does* belong to you, Frida, but it isn't your home. There's a difference. You mustn't forget that." She pinned Frida with a thoughtful look. "You girls can't stay here, you know."

"But why ever not? We were in the book of necessary guests!"

The lioness smiled. "Exactly, Frida. You're *guests*. And good guests always leave in the end—however much we might want them to stay. But you must never forget your way here. Palaces like this won't survive without guests like you."

The lioness was almost talking in riddles. Frida tried to understand, but before she could find out anything more, Saleem had strutted over to the table. "Do take your fill, my ladies," he said. "But leave some time for dancing. Princess Frida, will you do me the honor?"

"Dancing?" said Frida. She felt inexplicably sad after her conversation with the lioness. "Oh, I don't dance. I can't."

Saleem readjusted his waistcoat. "You can't dance? Don't believe it for a minute."

"None of us has ever really danced before."

"*Ever?*"

"Oh, well, there were the courtly dances we were taught as little girls: a step here, a heel there." Frida looked over to the dance floor. "But shimmying and stomping like those bears? Never."

Saleem extended his wing, and it flashed iridescent in the light. "So brave to come here, but she won't dance! Fear not, Princess Frida! I will take the utmost care of you. Michel the monkey is playing a solo on the saxophone, and it is not something I care to miss."

"Oh, go on, Frida," said Polina. "You need to let your hair down. You've looked after us so well. Go and have some fun."

"She's right!" said the others. "Please, Frida. Please dance with Saleem!"

Only for her sisters did she accept Saleem's invitation, but it was a dance that stayed inside her feet for the rest of Frida's life. As soon as the peacock and the princess took to the floor, it was clear that Saleem was an excellent dancer—wings neat, toes tidy, feathers adding the flair.

But it wasn't that.

It was the freedom Frida had talked of but never known for herself until now, until the endless music and movement, around in circles, hand in wing—sometimes on her own, her feet moving and stamping, arms in the air, body jumping and swirling, whirling and twirling, in and out of the multicolored lights. She felt as if her feet were flying on Saleem's wings, as if every soul on that dance floor with her—her eleven sisters, the lioness too, even a couple of the toucan waiters—had truly understood what it meant to be alive. And Frida said to herself, *What more could I ask from life than a monkey playing the sax, a stomach full of doughnuts, my sisters close, and a dance floor made for us inside the roots of a gigantic tree?*

But in that moment, the lioness came up and whispered hot breath into Frida's ear: "Even necessary guests must leave, my dear—and nothing in this palace comes for free."

Five

King Alberto's Second Bad Decision

It was the best time the sisters had ever known. Every night, their father would lock them in with his heavy iron key, and after the palace had fallen quiet, they would take turns pushing open the secret door behind their mother's portrait,

and down they would go,

all five hundred and three steps of the dark staircase,

across the lagoon,

through the three beauteous forests,

until finally they reached their tree palace, where the lioness would greet them at the arch, Saleem would show them to their regular table, and the toucan waiters would attend to their every happiness.

Whatever the girls had dreamed of eating, that exact dish was always on the menu. Baked beans on toast, spaghetti with clams, fresh fried fish in buttery buns? No matter what they'd been dreaming about on the way there, the lioness's kitchen was ready. She would sit with them, and they would talk to her about their dreams for the future, or they would tell silly jokes, and she would tell them stories about princesses locked in rooms. And then the girls would dance in rapture to the jazz music until they could barely feel their feet and their shoes were worn through.

And every morning in the upstairs palace, King Alberto would unlock their bedroom door to find his twelve lovely daughters fast asleep in their rows of beds. All the king had ever wanted was for his girls to go to sleep, because he believed that only in their dreams could they be safe. (That, and they were easier to manage than when they were awake.) As he watched them snoring, he was delighted that they were finally so obedient.

The girls hated their daytime hours of doing nothing. But

although the king and his advisers continued to deny them any tasks or pleasures, the existence of their tree palace made everything bearable. The sisters knew that, come the night, they would have a chance once more to feel free.

They would whisper about new dance steps, what tiara might look best with their pajamas. Ariosta looked forward to a swim in the lagoon. Delilah had discovered that the forests contained other plants for her to examine. Emelia always kept her eyes peeled for the little golden fox, but I am sad to say she never saw him again. Instead, she busied herself making sure the jazz musicians had sleek fur and clean claws, in order to play their instruments to the best of their abilities. Chessa, who had been promised an invitation by the lioness to sing onstage with the band, would practice in her mind which numbers she was going to perform.

In short, the girls started to feel alive. They were in possession of the most brilliant secret, and they hid it so very well that neither King Alberto nor any of his advisers had the faintest clue.

"It feels like *home*!" Bellina declared happily one breaking dawn, all of them sinking gratefully (but not particularly gracefully) into their beds after a night of dancing.

But Frida was worried. She'd never been able to put out of her mind what the lioness had told her on their first visit. The lioness had said that the tree palace *belonged* to the princesses, but they could never call it home. Was that because someone was going to steal it from them? Why was she so insistent on reminding Frida that they must leave the tree palace, when it seemed expressly designed for them? And if nothing in the tree palace came for free, what was the price they were going to have to pay for spending so much time there?

She almost felt anger at the lioness—for showing them such a wonderful place and making them feel as if it was theirs, only to suggest they couldn't stay. They'd explained to her how miserable their life upstairs had become! It wasn't as if the lioness was unaware of their horrid situation.

Frida sighed to herself. Her mother's death had taught her well that the world doesn't always skip along to your wishes. But then again, wisdom didn't always make this fact any easier to accept.

So one night, after coming back up the staircase at dawn, closing the secret door quietly, adjusting her mother's portrait, and making sure every princess was accounted for, Frida said they should make a pact. "We must swear to one another that we will protect this tree palace," she said, kicking off her worn-out shoes and rubbing the balls of her feet.

"But why? We're not going to tell anyone," said Ariosta, snuggling under her comforter.

"Of course we're not. But that might not stop Father's advisers—or Father himself—from asking questions."

"Father's none the wiser," said Flora. "We've been doing this for weeks!"

Frida frowned like a military general. "True, but we cannot be complacent. What would we do if we could never dance in the tree palace again? If we were trapped in this bedroom without even the promise of the music down below to cheer us up?"

"Imagine never seeing the lioness again!" said Delilah.

"Or Saleem," said Mariella.

"Ugh," said Vita, burying her face in her pillow. "I couldn't bear it."

"Exactly," said Frida. "We must plan. We found the tree palace together, and if anything happens we will defend it together. Whatever it takes, we'll do it. Agreed?" She put her hand out.

"Agreed," said the eleven others, without hesitation, piling their hands on top of Frida's.

But as it happened, there was just one tiny detail the girls hadn't thought through. Not even clever Frida.

It caught them out, as you might say, royally.

※

One morning, King Alberto opened their bedroom door as usual. And, as usual, his daughters' twelve pairs of shoes were lined up neatly against the wall. Except this time (Why this time? Who knows—kings are unreliable characters) he bent down and lifted one shoe in order to admire the craftsmanship.

The king was in for a shock.

He stood there in the soft morning light, shaking his gray head as his girls slumbered away. "These are not the shoes of a princess," he said to himself. "They're completely ruined!"

And he was right. The sole of this particular shoe—belonging, in this case, to Polina—was utterly destroyed. The king reached down and picked up another shoe, then another and another— until he'd turned all twenty-four shoes upside down.

All of them had more holes than a fine Swiss cheese.

He tiptoed away and ordered the royal shoemaker to make the girls some better ones.

"But I never stop making shoes for your daughters, Your Majesty," said the shoemaker.

"I beg your pardon?" said King Alberto.

The shoemaker gestured mournfully toward his dwindling leather supplies. "I've made more pairs of shoes for them than my wife makes me hot dinners."

"What on earth is going on?" King Alberto asked himself, for the shoemaker was a talented man and had been making sturdy footwear since the king was a boy.

The next morning, the king opened the girls' bedroom door and discovered that the shoes he'd ordered for his daughters but one day previously were again worn through.

He sent for even more shoes. And yet again, the morning after their delivery, while his daughters slept unawares, he found that every shoe was ruined.

King Alberto hated not knowing answers generally, but this particular mystery enraged him. You'd think a king had bigger fish to fry, but no! He summoned each daughter, one by one, and asked them to explain the reason behind the unending pairs of holey shoes. The girls were frightened, but Frida had prepared them for disaster. Remembering the pact they had made to one another, the princesses held their nerve.

"The guard dogs bite them," said Frida.

"I walk a great deal," said Polina.

"I stood on a nail," said Lorna.

"The shoemaker's no good," said Ariosta.

"My feet get hot, so I let the air in," said Chessa.

"I find mice in them," said Bellina. "We need to get a palace cat."

"It's my fault," laughed Vita. "I scuff my feet all day."

"I have no idea," said Mariella, with a shrug.

"I ripped them on a tree root in the garden," said Delilah.

"I held them too long over a candle when I was warming them up," said Flora.

"They're my favorite pair, so I've worn them through," said Emelia.

"Maybe they're supposed to have holes?" said Agnes, staring at the floor.

King Alberto was sure they weren't telling the truth. He felt it in his royal gut. His daughters had such innocent faces, but it was too bizarre that they were going through so many pairs of shoes at such a rapid rate! The shoemaker, who had made thousands of pairs of shoes and whose fingers were worn to the bone, begged for early retirement. The king dismissed him and raged that his daughters were out of control.

"They're just shoes, Your Majesty!" his advisers pleaded with him, knowing that there were much more important things to be worrying about, like gathering the harvests and the uprisings in the west of the kingdom.

The king couldn't agree. They weren't just *shoes*. They were his *daughters'* shoes, and they had holes in them when they shouldn't. It felt like his girls were going somewhere beyond his reach, and he didn't like it.

One morning, he summoned Frida to his throne.

Frida came, feeling a nervousness in her stomach that she tried to push away. As usual, the black drapes were up, but Frida could just make out the dust gathering in small gray balls around the legs of her father's ornate throne. *Really, someone should do a spring cleaning in here,* she thought.

Her father's advisers were huddled in the corner like a group of worried penguins, the candlelight throwing their shadows into grotesque shapes. She sighed, thinking about the beautiful multicolored lights of the tree palace, the fluttering wings of the toucan waiters, how pleased the lioness always was to see the princesses, and how they danced and danced with Saleem—

"So, my girl," the king said, interrupting her daydream. "Are you going to tell me your secret?"

Frida flicked her eyes toward the king. Something in her father's voice chilled her. The memories of the previous night's dancing melted like ice under a flame.

"My secret?" she echoed.

"Come on, Frida. You're slyer than a fox. You're the eldest. You're the ringleader. You should be setting an example. I've asked you all why your shoes are worn out and not one of you has told me the truth. Why are your sisters all so disobedient?"

Frida thought about her younger sisters. They were so much happier since the discovery of the tree palace: it made their life in this upstairs mausoleum tolerable. She thought of the pact she'd asked them to make. In a way, her father was right. She *was* responsible. She had been the one to find the door behind the painting, after all. She had been the first to shake the lioness's paw. She had been the one who encouraged her sisters to lie. "Father," she replied, "they are not disobedient. They are loyal and true."

"True to what?" asked her father. "To *whom*?"

Frida remained silent.

"You are the most disobedient of all," he said. "Just like your mother."

Frida closed her eyes. "I beg you, Father, attend to your kingship."

"Outrageous cheek! I will know your secret," Alberto raged, "and you will tell me or face the consequence!"

Frida took a deep breath. *The consequence.* She knew silence was no longer an option, that she must speak and suffer. "Father," she said quietly, "it is not your secret to know."

At this, the king leaped out of his throne, the hair on the top of his head quivering. The advisers rushed forward, worried that he might trip on his robes. "Get out!" he screamed at his daughter. "But don't think this is the end. I'll get the truth out of you if it's the last thing I do!"

For the first time in her life, Frida was truly frightened. Suddenly, the lioness's voice filled her ears: *Nothing in this palace comes for free.*

She looked at her father's advisers, who did nothing to help her, and she stumbled away, running through the gloom of the corridors to find her sisters. *You think I'm slyer than a fox?* she thought, her mind racing. She remembered the golden fox that Emelia had saved, down in the darkness. *Well, Father,* she thought. *And you too, lioness. You haven't seen anything yet.*

By the time Frida returned to the bedroom, she had composed herself.

"What did he say?" asked Vita, looking nervous.

"Nothing he hasn't said already," said Frida, smiling. "Don't worry. We'll go down to the tree palace tonight and have a marvelous time. Although—listen, my darlings. Look after the soles of your shoes. Less dancing, if possible."

She was met with a chorus of protest.

"I know, I know. But we need to be even cleverer than we already are."

Frida never wanted to be the one to tell her sisters to dance less. But what could she do? Their father was so suspicious, so dangerous! His face in anger these days was redder than a lobster. She feared that their time in the tree palace was running out, but she wasn't going to let her sisters worry too. She racked her brains to think of some way to put King Alberto off the scent, while ensuring her sisters could still go to the tree palace. Yet all the time, the lioness's words went around in her head: *Even necessary guests must leave.*

That night, as they rowed across the lagoon, Frida draped her fingers in the dark water. She felt its cool quality, how its very touch cleansed her father's anger and strengthened her resolve.

They walked through the forest of silver, with Frida bringing up the rear. Making sure none of the others saw her, Frida quietly picked up a shining fallen leaf and slipped it into the pocket of her dressing gown. When they reached the forest of gold, Frida did the same again, scooping up a glowing twig, adding it to the silver leaf. And in the forest of diamonds, ensuring that she was the last to leave, she plucked one of the precious stones and dropped it in her pocket. It rested with the silver leaf and gold tree limb, cold and hard through the fabric of her gown.

None of the other girls noticed a thing.

That night in the tree palace, the lioness decided the time had come for Chessa to step up to the stage and take her moment.

"Chessa," she announced, "you are our starriest singer, on this starriest night!"

The other girls clapped and cheered, delighted that the lioness was finally going to hear their sister's magical voice. Chessa, who had been waiting for this for weeks, bounded up, standing before the microphone as if it was the most comfortable place in the world.

Even the shimmying bears in their sequin skirts—even the toucan waiters—stopped what they were doing to listen. A hush fell, and Chessa began to sing. Into the silence, her beautiful, entrancing voice rose up, spreading through the roots of the tree. It wove like invisible smoke into the ear, filling their hearts, bringing tears to eyes and smiles to whiskers.

Oh, it was an evening none of them would ever forget. Chessa started with a song called "Laurelia, My Love," a sad number that nevertheless had some strains of happiness to be heard in its major shifts, but her next number was a jumpy, jivey, madcap extravaganza, with Michel the monkey on the saxophone, that had everyone whooping out of their chairs onto the dance floor.

Vita even taught the bears how to pirouette three times in a row without falling over. And every time Chessa thought her set was finished, trying to step away from the microphone in order to slug back a glass of elderflower fizz and reunite with her sisters, the leopard with his clarinet and the tabby cat on her trumpet would shout, "Come back and sing another!"—and the ostrich threw her feathers at Chessa's feet in adoration.

The lioness, who had noticed Frida looking a little sad despite all this fun, sat down next to her.

"Have you been thinking about what I said, Princess Frida?"

she asked in her low, warm voice. "Have you been thinking how to say goodbye?"

"I never stop thinking about it," said Frida, a little coldly. She felt the remnants she had taken from the three forests lodged inside the pocket of her dressing gown.

"You're angry with me," said the lioness.

Frida didn't dare admit it, but she could not help but speak a little of her mind. "But it's so *lovely* down here, you see?" she said. "My sisters are happy. Look at them dancing!"

The lioness twisted her whiskers together and let them spring apart again. "Tree palace or no tree palace, you and your sisters have a capacity to be happy wherever you are, which is a very fortunate thing indeed."

"Our father—" Frida began.

"From what you've told me about your father," said the lioness, "he does not sound like a bad man. But he is a lost one. Parents can be tricky creatures." She smiled at Frida. "Or so I've heard."

"Here is the only place we can feel happy," said Frida, feeling stubborn.

The lioness turned away from the chaos on the dance floor

and placed a dinner-plate paw on Frida's heart. "No, Frida, that's not true," she said. "Look closer."

"He wants to know what we're doing every night to make our shoes so worn out. He keeps summoning me, talking about *the consequence*. I'm scared what he'll do if he finds out—"

"*Frida.*" The lioness pressed a little harder with her paw, and Frida felt suffused with such serene power, such warmth and contentment, such a sense of coming home.

"I promise you, I understand," the lioness said. "But listen to me. Frida, trust yourself. You know exactly what you have to do."

✳

The next morning, King Alberto summoned his eldest daughter yet again.

He looked crazed. His hair was even more stuck out through the top of his crown, and he was waving a pair of Frida's shoes on his hands. "Do these look like the shoes of a princess?" he shouted.

Frida had felt completely calm since her conversation with the lioness at the end of the previous evening. Her whispered words made circles in her head: *Frida, trust yourself.*

85

"They look like the shoes of a woman with places to go," she said to her father.

"Argh!" King Alberto hurled the shoes across the room, where they struck the side of an adviser's head with a leathery slap. "You have *nowhere* to go," her father cried. "And I made it so in order to protect you!"

"You have let us rot inside this palace," she replied. "You've been so scared that we will die, as your queen has died, that you've tried to stop us from living. You're mad with grief and blind to your madness. It has been outrageous and unfair."

He narrowed his eyes. "Then tell me your secret, and maybe I'll give you some freedom."

She looked him in the eye. "I fear your idea of freedom is not the same as mine."

"Frida, as your king, I demand the secret."

She took a deep breath. "Then, as your subject, I deny you."

"Then you give me no choice," her father roared.

Frida knew that *the consequence* was coming.

"Frida, I banish you!"

She bowed her head. The air sang with a strange electricity.

I banish you. Her father's words washed over her, they drenched her skin with pain, but they did not unsteady her. She did not move, she did not speak. *Banished*: the word like a magic spell! Out of the corner of her eye, Frida could see the advisers, frozen in fear. From far off, she was certain she heard a lion's cry.

"Sire," said one of the advisers, stepping out of the shadows, clutching the hurled shoes. He cleared his throat. It was Clarence, the youngest of Alberto's staff, a pair of shrewd eyes in that whippety-thin face. Despite his youth, Clarence looked exhausted, as if dealing with Alberto over the past weeks had done him in.

"Princess Frida is—um, a great *asset* to Kalia, Your Majesty. Are you quite sure that this is a—er, a sensible thing to do?"

"Be quiet!" screamed Alberto. "Only weaklings change their minds! Frida, did you hear me? You're *banished*!"

Still Frida did not speak. The king stopped, catching his breath. "And hear this too," he went on, clambering out of his throne and pacing up and down. "Whosoever can solve the riddle of your sisters' shoes shall inherit my kingdom and choose any remaining girl for a wife."

"Sire!" cried Clarence.

87

But King Alberto was past listening to counsel. He pointed to the circle of gold resting on his hair. "And I shall place this crown on their head myself."

Again, Frida said nothing, her eyes fixed on the balls of dust around her father's throne. The king's own eyes widened as he circled around her. "Oh, you've nothing to say now, Frida? Thought not—it's a miracle—Frida has nothing to say! This is my royal decree," he spat. "And once done, it cannot be undone. Didn't you say I was the law?"

At this, Frida looked up. She could feel the chill of the silver forest running through her veins and how the heat of the gold forest was turning the inside of her head to flames. She looked at her father, and her eyes flashed as hard as a pair of diamonds. Clarence shrank from her, and King Alberto looked frightened.

"See how he would give away a daughter so thoughtlessly?" she said. Her voice was strong and clear. "Never mind the kingdom. Of *course* it's not sensible, Clarence. But when has my father ever done anything sensible?" She drew herself up. "Father, you can banish me, but to marry one of my sisters to a man she does not love—that is beyond cruelty."

"My word is final!" said King Alberto.

Frida looked at him with a thoughtful expression she had borrowed from the lioness. "I see that you will never change the way you treat your daughters. It pains me. Perhaps you will live to regret it. But even after this, for as long as you call me daughter, I will never tell you the secret of our shoes."

Alberto climbed back up into his throne and thumped his fist on the arm. "Then I shall never call you daughter again!"

Frida took her shoes from Clarence's thin and trembling hands. "Then so it shall be," she said, and walked from the throne room without another word.

✳

Frida's sisters were enjoying their hour in the palace grounds, still unaware of her predicament. She took a pouch of Kalian coins from the royal mint, and packed the meager contents of her drawers into a suitcase as quickly as she could. She added the silver leaf, glittering with light, the gold branch that glowed like the sun, and the single diamond, hard and cold in her palm, plucked from her last visit to the underground world.

When her sisters came back, they found a pale-faced Frida sitting on the edge of her bed, in a plain brown dress and the sort of coat that no one would ever suppose belonged to a princess.

"Where on earth did you find that coat?" asked Delilah.

"And why do you have a suitcase?" asked Mariella.

"It's Father, isn't it?" Agnes said.

"It's always Father," said Ariosta.

Frida smiled sadly. "He's realized that there's another reason why our shoes are wearing out so quickly, and he wants to know what it is, of course. He wants to know about Saleem and the lioness and the toucan waiters. He wants to know it all. But I won't tell him any of it. So here's the thing, my loves. He's banished me."

A cry came up from the others, a sound of rage and sadness.

"*Banished?*" said Bellina, falling to the floor, wrapping her arms around Frida's knees. "No, no, you can't leave us, you *can't*."

"You'll be perfectly fine without me," said Frida.

"We won't," said Polina.

"Where will you go?" said Lorna.

"How are you going to *survive*?" asked Flora.

"I was born to do more than survive. And so were you." Frida rummaged in her coat pocket and pulled out a key. "And guess what I've got."

"*No*. It can't be," said Vita. "You naughty thing!"

"The key to Mother's motor car." Frida grinned. "If Father thinks I'm walking out of here, or riding a *horse*, he's in for a surprise."

"I think you're lucky," said Emelia. "You get to leave. You get true freedom, while the rest of us stay here."

The others were quiet at this, and Frida looked somber. She thought about the terrible decree her father was going to make, how he would give one of his daughters away, and his kingdom too, to whichever man—it didn't even matter who he was!—as long as he was first to uncover the secret. Emelia was right in that respect, Frida thought. By being banished from Kalia, a random marriage against her will was one fate she was definitely going to avoid. King Alberto was indeed a law unto himself; look at the way he treated even clever Clarence. Her sisters were going to have to be strong.

Frida stood up. "I'm lucky in some ways, Emmy," she said. "But you'll still have the tree palace. It will be there for as long as you need it. More importantly, you still have each other. And anyway, I've a suspicion that freedom is a bit of a slippery fish." She placed her hand on each of their hearts, one after the other, just as the lioness had done to her. "I swear to you, as I love each and every one of you, I *will* come back."

She scooped her suitcase off the bed. "I don't know where I'm going, but I promise that I will work out how to free us all. In the meantime, you must never stop going down to the tree palace. Do you promise? You have to keep going, otherwise . . . well, otherwise it might just disappear."

"Disappear? How?" asked Chessa.

"If a tree palace doesn't have its necessary guests, it might get forgotten. If you want to keep something alive, you have to turn up."

"We will," said Agnes. "We promise."

"There are going to be difficult times ahead," said Frida. "So cry if you feel like crying. Never hold in tears; it's pointless. Then dry your eyes, look around you, think—think a bit *more*—then act. It's time to stand on your own twenty-two feet, my loves, whether your shoes have holes in them or not. And if you can cross lagoons and heal foxes and find tree palaces, then you're halfway there already."

She hugged each of her sisters tightly. "Will you tell the lioness that I understand now, and that I said goodbye?"

Before the princesses could ask Frida what she meant, she had gripped her suitcase handle and walked out of the bedroom with her head held high. She took a left, then a right toward the staircase that led to the palace garages.

The royal mechanic, who'd heard about the banishment and assumed she was there under her father's orders, opened the garage door for her. Frida revved her mother's engine so loudly that the mice, who had been happily nesting in the passenger seat for several generations by now, squeaked in terror, jumped out en masse, and dived inside an empty gas can.

Her sisters, who, as you will recall, had no window in their room, couldn't even watch her go.

Frida drove along the coastal road out of Lago Puera, the salt wind billowing her loose hair, the sun on her back, both palaces diminishing with every revolution of Laurelia's wheels. Who knew that standing up to her father would give her the freedom she'd so desired? That part had been easy in the end, but it didn't make it any easier to leave.

The truth was, Frida's feelings were complicated.

Look at this sunshine—this should have been a glorious

moment, something she'd longed for for years! But how could she be happy knowing her sisters were at the mercy of their father's ridiculous decree?

Frida sighed, set her eyes on the road, and knew that she would never dance in the tree palace again. The lioness had known this day would come, well before Frida had. But the tree palace had not completely disappeared. It was inside Frida now, a paw-print pressure, a hot-coal memory stoking her fire. And her sisters would

still go dancing. They must; it was all they had. They would think of something to protect their secret, and so would she.

A few more turns of the wheels, and the motor car dipped over the brow of a hill.

Frida honked her horn at the last of the Kalian seagulls,

and with that, the eldest princess crossed the city border,

and was gone.

Six

Delilah and the Dormidon

Meanwhile, back at the palace, King Alberto printed his ridiculous decree one thousand times. It looked like this:

ROYAL DECREE

ATTENTION, SUBJECTS:

BE THE MAN WHO SOLVES THE SECRET OF THE SHOES!

INHERIT THE KINGDOM OF KALIA AND MARRY A PRINCESS

(I'VE GOT ELEVEN: YOU CAN CHOOSE)

Interested candidates: please register at the main palace door

by Tuesday morning

By order of HM King Alberto of the Kingly Kingdom of Kalia

Signed: Alberto Rex

One thousand decrees were glued fast to shop windows and café doors, and farther afield, on farmers' gates. The kingdom and its princesses were up for grabs, and King Alberto wanted everyone to know. Some of the decrees came unstuck, and I like to think of them being blown by the sea winds far beyond the city, along the coast road, up over the hills, and onto the mountain passes. I also like to think that one found its way into Frida's hands. One can only imagine her feelings on seeing her father's stupidity, proved in print.

By Tuesday, a long line of applicants appeared outside the palace door. Men of all ages and abilities came to try their luck in solving the mystery of the princesses' shoes. They arrived from every corner of the kingdom, far beyond the city of Lago Puera: from the borderlands, from the mountains, from the sand-dune towns. Some women came too, but to their intense annoyance, the palace guards told them to leave.

The men formed an orderly queue, flexing their muscles at one another and boasting about which girl they'd pick out of the remaining eleven. They set up tents, and market traders came to sell them lunch, and street entertainers came to take their money. None of these men had much idea what was actually going

to be asked of them once they were inside the palace walls. They just knew it was something about shoes, so it was going to be easy.

Clarence, the whippety-thin adviser, slipped behind one of the black drapes over the throne room window and watched the circus gather. He thought King Alberto had lost his mind. Princess Frida had been right—what sort of method was this to find the future king of Kalia? Alberto had ordered that a camp bed be set up outside the girls' room for a man to sleep on. Rightly anticipating a high level of interest, he'd decreed that each man would be allowed one night only to solve the mystery.

Clarence put his face in his hands and hoped for a miracle.

The eleven remaining sisters, who had been allowed into the throne room as these events unfolded, watched miserably from another window. Bellina threw a walnut and snickered as it bounced off a man's head.

"I don't care if these men are princes or paupers; I don't want any of them," said Ariosta.

"This is *awful*," said Lorna. "I feel sick. I miss Frida so much."

"Frida said she'd come back and save us, and I believe her," said Agnes.

But the other girls could not share their youngest sister's hope. Vita's usually happy face was pale. "Well, she isn't here now, and we're going to have to be very, very clever," she said.

"You're right. All sorts of idiots are going to try to uncover our secret," said Delilah. "We have to make sure none of them succeeds, but we are *not* going to throw walnuts." She gave Bellina a stern look.

"Frida was banished for refusing to reveal our secret," Chessa whispered. "She sacrificed her happiness for ours. So we must never stop"—here, she mouthed the word—"*dancing.*"

"That would make Frida's banishment twice as bad," agreed Ariosta. "The tree palace is all we have now. I wonder where she is. Will she write to us, do you think?"

Mariella was sobbing quietly. "I don't want to get married," she said.

"I certainly don't want to marry anyone so intent on spoiling our fun," said Polina, looking out of the window at the line of preening men.

"Exactly—someone who's going to peer through the keyhole and creep behind us, watching everything we do," said Agnes with a shudder. "Anyway, I'm too young to be married. Surely if I'm ever picked, Father will say no?"

Lorna bit her lip. "I don't know, Aggie. That is why we have to be careful."

"But, girls," said Flora. "Whichever man comes to sit outside our door, he'll know we're not in there. We can't block up the keyhole, because he'll get suspicious. What are we going to *do*?"

The princesses looked forlornly at one another as, outside, the line of men grew and grew. Their situation felt impossible. It seemed inevitable that one of them—someday soon—would be taken as a reluctant bride and the rest of them forbidden to dance ever again.

Suddenly, Delilah's eyes widened in excitement. "Oh, boy. I've got it," she said. "Why didn't I think of this before? Bedroom. Now, before the first man gets in."

As princessly as they could, the eleven girls walked back to their room. They could almost see the excitement fizzing around Delilah's head.

Once they were all inside, and the bedroom door closed, Delilah rushed over to her dressing gown. From down below, they could hear the palace door being opened and the sound of tramping feet as the men lined up to be registered to sleep outside the princesses' room.

"It's got to be here somewhere," Delilah said, throwing leaves and soil and even a wood louse across her bed. "Aha!" She brandished her treasure at her sisters. It didn't look very promising: a limp, dried vine of brownish color, dangling from her hands like a worm.

"That's supposed to help us?" said Bellina, tears welling in her eyes.

"Yes, it is," said Delilah proudly. "Don't you remember the first time we went to the tree palace?" Her sisters looked at her blankly. "The *dormidon*!" she whispered. "All right," she said, hoisting herself up onto her bed and looking around at her sisters. "I know it doesn't look like much. But we haven't much time, and we need to discuss this. Tell me what you know about the dormidon plant."

No one said anything. Delilah sighed. Voices could be heard coming up the corridor.

"Delilah, *hurry*," said Agnes.

"Girls, we *are* going to go dancing," Delilah said. She held the vine up. "And this is how: If you drop a dormidon vine in hot water and drain off the liquid, it will make you a tasteless sleeping draft so powerful that just one drop of it in a goblet of wine or cup of tea is enough to knock a grown man out for twelve hours." Her voice dropped to a whisper. "But you have to be very, very careful with the dormidon, because too much of it will kill someone. Only experienced botanists should handle such a powerful little plant."

"An experienced botanist like you, say?" said Agnes, grinning.

Delilah grinned back. "You know exactly where this is going, don't you, Aggie. I've got enough in this bedroom for a hundred men."

"But what if you make a mistake and knock them out . . . forever?" said Emelia.

"Well, it's their own fault for coming here to ruin our lives in the first place," said Ariosta. "Spying on us, trying to marry us without our permission."

"I'd put three dormidons in their drink if I could," said Vita.

Lorna put up her hands. "All right, all right. We don't want dead men on our hands. We just want them to leave us alone."

"Wise to pursue?" Delilah asked her sisters.

"Wise to pursue," they whispered back.

The first man to be admitted was—how can I put this tactfully?—a buffoon. He didn't walk into the palace; he *swaggered*. He practically *rolled* in, as if grabbing the kingdom for himself and picking a daughter—or grabbing a daughter and picking the kingdom—was as easy as brushing his teeth.

I forget his name. It doesn't matter.

It was Agnes, the most innocent-looking, the sweetest, the most childlike, who smiled and handed him a good-night cup of milky

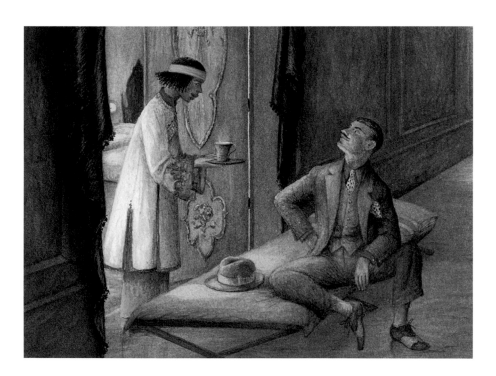

hot chocolate as he sat on the edge of the camp bed. The man took it greedily, not even bothering to say thank you before he swigged it down. The girls were locked in their room immediately after.

Settling in for a night of vigilance, he was asleep in five minutes.

✳

That night in the tree palace, every one of the princesses danced that little bit longer, taking extra pleasure in every whirl and jig they made, in case it was the last time they might ever be allowed. Agnes told the lioness that Frida wanted her to know that she understood, and passed on her message of goodbye. The youngest princess was surprised by the look of pride in the lioness's eyes, where Agnes thought there might at least have been sadness.

The next morning, Delilah's plan had worked.

The first man was late to his meeting with the king and had no evidence to present him as to the girls' activity. He could barely string a sentence together and was booted out of the first-floor window, and—if I recall correctly, from Emelia's account of it—he landed slap-bang in a pile of horse manure.

The second man was given a goblet of delicious Kalian wine to drink. Again, Agnes, the saintly darling little angel that she was,

was given the job of handing over the drink. He sloshed it down, and through their door the girls could hear his teeth clanking against the soft gold of the cup, followed by loud snoring. They moved aside their mother's portrait and vanished in silence.

That night, down in the tree palace, they told Saleem and the lioness the news. Delilah was made guest of honor, and the toucans brought her a special doughnut filled with wild blueberry jam, with a diamond on top.

✳

"It's all right," said King Alberto to himself, after the third, the fourth, the fifth, the sixth man entered the palace, full of confidence, only to be dismissed as unsuccessful, unable to recall a jot of what he might have seen or heard. "There are enough men out there. One of them will crack it, I'm sure."

By the failure of the eightieth man, King Alberto was nearly bursting with fury.

Over the next four months, the line outside the palace shrank as, one by one, the men attempted to uncover the secret of the shoes and, one by one, they failed. Their tents were packed up, the smell of street food evaporated, and the entertainers left to find bigger audiences in other kingdoms. Inside the palace, King Alberto bounced up and down on his throne until his backside split a cushion. "Does every man in Kalia have a radish for a brain?" he ranted, spluttering on the feathers.

His advisers, particularly Clarence, were delighted that Alberto's scheme was failing, but the girls didn't know how much longer they could get away with drugging a man with dormidon every night. Delilah's supply of the plant was running perilously low. The last time they'd gone to the forest of diamonds, they realized they'd plucked all the ripe plants, and the saplings were still growing.

But while they still had the last of the dormidon to help them, the eleven sisters descended the five hundred and three steps of the staircase, crossed the lagoon in their boats, walked through the three sparkling forests, and danced in their tree palace until their shoes had lost their soles. Saleem and the lioness were always happy to see them, but they always asked them if they had news of Frida, and the sisters always had to say no. The telephone lines were still disconnected, and they hadn't even received a letter.

And were they happy?

Well, that's a good question. Their happiness these days was of a strange kind. They were outsmarting those who wanted to ruin their fun, but it was a happiness that lasted in the whirl of a dance and died within a breath. It was *tiring*, having to attend to these men every day. And it wasn't just that. Going to bed in the early hours of morning, they felt as if an anchor of sadness was plunging through them, pinning them to their mattresses. The dancing had stopped being enough. They dearly missed their sister. They wanted her stories, her strength. They wanted to stand on their twenty-four feet together, not their twenty-two.

Eventually, the last man turned his back on the palace, thwarted in his attempt to unmask the princesses' secret. The king was exhausted, regretting deeply that he'd ever agreed to such a ridiculous scheme. He blamed his advisers for suggesting it, and they duly apologized.

For the girls, never had a victory tasted so bittersweet. A bit like pre-boiled dormidon, in fact.

The palace was quiet. None of the girls felt like dancing. Not even a tiny jig.

And then, just like that, everything in Kalia changed forever.

Seven

A Coronation

It was Vita who heard it first: a faint buzzing in the sky. It was coming, she suspected, from across the sea.

It was their hour of recreation, and the eleven girls were in the palace garden, wandering aimlessly among the palms and hothouse flowers, whose bright pinks no longer cheered them. The high walls that surrounded them cut most of the sunshine at this time of day, and the garden had no view.

But Vita heard it, all the same. She looked up and saw only the bright rectangle of cloudless blue above her. Yet the buzzing was getting louder. "Ariosta," she said to her sister, "give me a leg up against that wall."

"I beg your pardon?"

"*Listen.* Can't you hear that?"

"It's just an angry bee."

"Don't be ridiculous. No bee is ever that angry. I want to see!"

In the end, it took Emelia standing on Flora, standing on Delilah, standing on Mariella, standing on Vita, standing on Bellina, standing on Chessa, standing on Ariosta, standing on Lorna, standing on Polina—with Agnes, who was the smallest, at the top on Emelia's shoulders—even to be able to *peer* over the top of the wall, taking a few precious seconds before the guards came back and all of them tumbled to the ground.

"What is it?" hissed Polina. "Please hurry up—my shoulders are killing me!"

"Oh my, oh *my*," said Agnes. "It's an airplane."

"Is that all? I think I'd rather it was an angry bee."

"No you wouldn't, Pol—this one's about to land on the beach!"

Agnes scaled down her sisters' arms and legs and ran out of the garden to find a better view. The others followed, the plane's engines reverberating deep in their bodies. No one stopped them, because by now everyone had heard that a plane was trying to land on the royal beach, and the palace was in an uproar, maids running hither and thither, advisers reaching for their robes, the guards trying to find their weapons. Nothing this exciting had happened in Kalia for *ages*.

From a high balcony, the princesses looked down and saw a small biplane circling above the turquoise surf. Whoever was flying it was an expert pilot, making circles and ovals, dipping down and soaring up into the sky. It was as if the pilot wanted to make sure that everyone in Lago Puera had seen this display, and the eleven princesses in particular, seeing as this was happening directly outside the palace. Eventually, it was time for the plane to land properly, and the girls watched its tail scud away before it turned around and came down upon the vast, empty stretch of royal sand that ribboned around the palace. The pilot landed effortlessly, with a single bump, and cut the engines.

The sisters watched with an exquisite mixture of excitement and dread as the palace guards rushed toward the aircraft, their revolvers at the ready. A group of advisers, led by Clarence, hurried after them. The cockpit window opened, and a tall, slender young man pushed his arms up, then his body, then his legs, before jumping down easily onto the sand. He was wearing a pilot's jumpsuit, a flying jacket, a white scarf, a leather cap, and a pair of goggles, but even with these covering his face, the princesses could see he was handsome.

They strained their ears to hear the conversation taking place on the beach. The pilot had pushed his goggles up onto his forehead and was now shading his eyes against the punishing sun as he admired the sea. "What a beautiful beach," he said. "Is this the kingdom of Kalia?"

"It might be," said Clarence. "Why do you want to know?"

The pilot fumbled in his jacket pocket and produced a piece of paper, which fluttered in the breeze. He steadied himself against the wing. "I'm here to see the king," he said. "King Alberto, I believe?"

"Oh, *no*," said Polina. "He's holding one of Father's decrees!"

Bellina groaned. "I thought we'd seen the last of those silly men."

"But he's so handsome," said Chessa. "And he's got a *plane*."

"I don't care if he's handsome! I don't care if he's got twenty planes! We still have to make him drink the dormidon!" said Ariosta, crossing her arms. "Turning up here with one of those dratted pieces of paper—"

"Of course, sweetest," said Polina, but she also found it rather hard to draw her eyes from the youth, who was by now walking in the center of the guards, striding up the beach, leaving nimble boot prints in the sand.

"Imagine dancing with *him*," breathed Agnes. "Oof, I bet he's an excellent dancer."

✳

The sisters hid behind a curtain and listened as the pilot spoke with their father.

"And where are you from?" King Alberto asked him.

"From across the sea," the pilot replied. Now that they were closer to him, the girls could hear his voice properly. It was low and calm, and ever so slightly musical.

"You've got a nice, um . . . airplane," said King Alberto. He sounded very un-king-like. (He'd given up hope, you understand—and it's not often you see someone so fine looking, so confident, someone who looks so perfectly like your future heir.) Alberto felt as if he was looking at one of his heroes from the fairy tales he'd read as a little boy. And a pilot, no less. How modern, how daring, to live up in the air!

"Thank you," said the youth, smiling. "In my kingdom, we guard our vehicles well—for battle, mainly."

"Been in any battles, have you?"

"Of sorts. My people fight a particular type of war."

"Excellent. And d'you hunt?"

"I have chased illusions, Your Majesty."

King Alberto nodded, pretending he'd understood. He'd never met such an impressive fellow. "Of course," he replied. "And I assume you're here to see if you can uncover the secret of my daughters' shoes?"

The youth handed over the crumpled decree. "I am."

"It'll take a miracle. My daughters have cleared this town of men."

"Well, miracles happen. And is it still true, sire, that you will crown me if I am successful?"

The king spread his hands. "But of course! A king never goes back on his word. Moreover, it's time for my retirement. And you would do perfectly, a good strapping lad like you. You're not . . . a prince, by any chance?"

The man bowed. "A royal since birth, Your Majesty."

The king clapped with joy. "Oh, marvelous, marvelous!" he cried. Clarence craned his neck with new interest toward the young man. King Alberto patted the pilot on the back and went off humming, thinking about the hobbies he would take up once he was no longer king.

✳

That night, Delilah prepared the last of the dormidon in the girls' little bathroom. And, as usual, Agnes was the one to offer it to the young pilot, this time in a glass of sweet mint tea. The pilot was sitting upright on the camp bed, his back against the wall. He looked thoughtful, and a little sad, his gaze cast toward the floor as he turned the glass of tea around and around in his hands. He wouldn't look at her, but Agnes was used to this by now—so few of the men who'd come to find their secret had bothered to acknowledge her. But this one hadn't looked at any

117

of the princesses as they'd filed past him; instead, he'd kept his chin down, half his face tucked in his scarf, deep in thought, eyes averted.

Agnes stood in front of him. "It's very good tea," she said. "You should drink it."

"Thank you," he mumbled into the scarf.

"Well, go on then. Drink it up."

"You seem very keen for me to drink this tea, Princess Agnes," he said, looking into the glass. Fragrant steam rose off the top of the liquid.

"I—" said Agnes.

"Do you like it here, Agnes?" the pilot asked.

"I . . . used to."

"Why?"

"Because we used to do experiments, and play music, and explore. Of course, we still have the—" Agnes stopped herself just in time. She'd found it strangely easy to talk to this pilot, but if any of her sisters heard her nearly reveal the tree palace, they'd be furious.

"You still have the secret," the pilot said, attempting to finish

118

her sentence. "You've guarded it well. From what I've heard, I'm about the thousandth person to try to uncover it." He laughed, and Agnes couldn't help grinning.

"Maybe," she said.

"And do you like being a princess?" the pilot asked.

"Bits of it."

"What bits?"

Agnes shifted from foot to foot. None of the other men had ever asked her any questions, and she wasn't used to it. "I like being with my sisters," she said. "But you want to take one of us away."

"Well, I would hope one day you'd leave this palace of your own will. There's a big world out there, Princess Agnes," the pilot said. "I've seen a bit of it. It wouldn't be so bad to go and take a look, you know."

Agnes was confused by this and grateful that, without another word, the young pilot put the glass to his lips and drank down the whole of the dormidon.

In a few minutes, the girls heard his light breathing. As they listened to the gentle slumber of the pilot on the other side of the

door, they felt strangely peaceful. And after Agnes told them what the pilot had said to her, for the first time in ages, the princesses truly wanted to dance.

✳

The next morning, they agreed that although it was a relief the dormidon had worked, it was a shame the young man would be on his way. They went down to the throne room to watch him be dismissed. He was dressed in his pilot's outfit and goggles and was holding a small sack at his side. Agnes noticed that his hands were trembling a little.

"So, my boy," King Alberto said. "Are you going to tell me the secret?"

At these words, the young man seemed to hesitate, but then resolved himself. "Yes, Your Majesty," he said. "I am."

The girls gasped. They all turned to Delilah. The dormidon had *worked*, hadn't it? Agnes said she'd watched him drink the whole thing! And they'd heard him snoring on the other side of the door! What on earth was going on? Delilah looked more boiled than the dormidon vine she'd prepared the night before.

King Alberto could hardly believe his ears. He leaned forward. "You *are?* Go on then. Spill the magic beans!"

"Your girls go dancing every night," the young man said.

"*What?*"

Agnes let out a cry, but the pilot carried on. "They open a secret door that lies behind the portrait of your wife in their bedroom."

Alberto's eyes boggled. "My wife's *portrait?*"

"Indeed, sir. One might say that Queen Laurelia leads the way. They go down five hundred and three steps, through the gloom and the cobwebs, toward a wide lagoon. Your daughter Ariosta swims into the deep water to find six little boats that the girls row over to the other side. They walk through three forests that they found themselves: The first is a forest of silver, which your daughter Chessa discovered. The second, which Emelia found when she helped a wounded fox, is made of gold. And the last is made of diamonds. In the forest of diamonds, you'll find the dormidon vine, which your botanist daughter, Delilah, has been using to drug all the suitors who have competed for your kingdom."

King Alberto looked toward his daughters in astonishment. "Ariosta?" he said dumbly. "I didn't even know you could swim. Chessa? Delilah, have you been . . . drugging a potential *king*?"

The girls stared with hatred at the pilot, but the pilot wasn't finished. "At the end of the forests, Your Majesty, they enter a tree palace."

At these words, several of the princesses fell to their knees.

"A *what*?" said King Alberto.

One of the older advisers, a man called Bernard, began to move forward. "Sire," he whispered in the king's ear. "This is preposterous. Shall we remove the young man now?"

"Your Majesty," said Clarence, looking with great interest at the pilot. "May I suggest it wiser to let him speak?"

The pilot carried on before the king could decide. "The tree palace is a dance floor in the roots of a tree, where your daughters dance and dine and sing with a lioness and a peacock and all kinds of other animals. They dance to their hearts' content. Their happiness is unlike any I've ever seen. And if I could bottle that happiness up, Your Majesty, I reckon I could fly my plane on it."

"This is absurd," said Bernard.

"But is it true?" asked the king.

"As true as I stand before you now. At the end of the evening, they return the way they came. They fall into bed, and they leave their shoes in a neat row, worn to pieces. And that, Your Majesty, is the sum total of the secret you have been craving all this time."

In the silence that followed, the princesses looked at one another in deep sorrow. The advisers would find the secret door. Their lives would be over. Their father would seal up the staircase, and after this, they would never be allowed out of their bedroom, even for an hour. And who was the pilot going to pick for a wife? Nobody liked him now. Lorna began to weep.

The king looked stunned. "A forest made of silver?" he said. "A forest made of gold?"

"He imagined it," said Bernard.

The pilot laughed. "Maybe I did. But it's real."

"Do you take His Majesty for a fool?" said Bernard. "There is no such thing as a tree palace, or dancing with a lioness. A lioness would eat you."

The pilot bowed. "Forgive me, but this particular lioness would not. Although," he added, looking Bernard up and down, "she might have a go at you."

"Pilot," said Clarence. "Do you have any proof of these forests? Then at least the matter can be settled."

The pilot bent down and opened the sack, and to the girls' horror he pulled out a single silver leaf, unmistakably from the forest. He pointed it at the king, and it shimmered in his hand like a small shield. King Alberto shrank back into the seat of his throne, a little frightened. The pilot put the silver leaf on the floor and pulled out a branch, made of gold. It glittered in the daylight, and he held it up to the king as if it were a ceremonial mace. The king swallowed nervously. And finally, the pilot rummaged in the sack and pulled out a large diamond. He handed it to Alberto, and it winked in his palm like an accusing eye.

"My goodness," breathed Alberto. "I've never seen precious metals like it. Girls, do you deny this? Answer me!"

Polina rose from the floor. Something in her looked broken. "Oh, Father," she said. "We only liked a little dancing!"

"Please, please, Father," said Vita. "*Please* don't lock us up again!"

The king lurched to his feet. "So it's true! Your insolence, your disobedience, your downright *outrageous* rebellion makes me sad to call you my daughters! Every night, going down to a dark lagoon, strange forests, talking lionesses—after all I did to try to keep you safe!"

The princesses looked at the pilot, their faces portraits of pure distress. "I understand it was precious to you, ladies," said the pilot. "Believe me. But the kingdom of Kalia needs a new ruler, so I really had no choice."

"How could you?" said Flora. "We thought you were *nice*!"

King Alberto turned to the pilot. *"Finally!"* he cried. "I've found someone worthy to inherit my kingdom! So clever, so brave, so ingenious! Come here, boy. You are a true prince and you shall have your reward. Clarence, see to it that the coronation takes place tomorrow. A small affair. No fuss."

The advisers looked at one another. Half of them, including Clarence, seemed to say, *Why not?* Alberto had always been an impossible king to manage one way or another, and this young man had excellent potential. The other half, led by Bernard, did

126

not look convinced. In fact, they looked very unhappy indeed, and stared at the boy with hostility.

"Are you sure you wish to crown me, sire?" asked the youth.

"I've never been surer of anything in my life!" replied the king. "And which one of these girls do you want for a wife?"

The pilot faltered, turning to the eleven girls, who scowled at him in unison. Agnes thought she saw a look of dismay pass across his face, which he quickly tried to hide.

"I'm not sure I'll ever know how to pick," he said.

Alberto beamed. "Crown first, bride later?" he asked the pilot.

"That couldn't be more perfect," came the young man's reply.

Clarence was an efficient organizer. The coronation was prepared for the next day, in the throne room. King Alberto even ordered the black drapes to be removed and the dust balls to be swept away from the legs of his throne. The maids had done a fabulous job cleaning the place, and the crystal chandelier sparkled in the glorious light.

There was just one small problem.

Unbeknownst to the pilot, or King Alberto and the eleven

girls, Bernard, the most suspicious of the king's advisers, decided to check whether the pilot's story was true: namely that, behind Laurelia's portrait, he would find a door that led down five hundred and three steps to a wide lagoon, three forests, and a tree palace. Once the princesses were in the throne room downstairs, Bernard snuck into the girls' cell and wrenched the portrait of Queen Laurelia from the wall.

There was no sign of a door.

Bernard looked and looked. He tapped the wall; he ran his hands over its stone—but he couldn't find a thing.

All he could see was a solid wall.

It was a trick! To think the future of Kalia was to be handed over like this to a complete stranger, and a liar at that! About what else had the pilot deceived them? "Never trust a man who arrives by plane," Bernard muttered to himself as he scurried furiously out of the girls' bedroom and through the palace to tell King Alberto, before it was too late.

The eleven princesses were, by now, seated on gold chairs to the left of the throne, with the advisers in favor of the pilot's coronation standing behind them. Alberto was sitting in the throne, a seat in which he had sat for years, and which he was soon to vacate. The king had even woken up his old herald, who hadn't played his trumpet since the passing of Queen Laurelia. He stood at Alberto's side, his trumpet waiting. There was an atmosphere of intense expectation.

When the pilot entered the throne room, a hush descended. Alberto stood up and removed the crown from his own head.

From far off, somewhere in the palace, came the sound of hurried footsteps.

The pilot approached the throne. As he knelt before Alberto, the girls could hardly breathe. The herald blew on his trumpet: a triumphant, trilling fanfare with suitably royal pomp.

The hurried footsteps were getting louder, reverberating along the corridor.

Alberto lifted the crown high. "With this, I name you King of Kalia," he said to the pilot, and the old man encircled the young man's head with the heft of the crown.

"Stop!" cried a voice, and Bernard burst into the throne room. Everyone turned to him. "There isn't any door!"

But Bernard was seconds too late. Kalia had a new king.

Clarence breathed an audible sigh, his thin face flushed with relief.

Agnes turned to the windows. The sea wind was blowing freshly through, the curtains danced in joy, and the sunlight in the room had become, yes, *brighter*. She blinked. Was that— was that—a *toucan* that just flew by? When she looked again, it was gone.

The adviser Bernard clung to the curtains, severely out of breath.

"And once done, it cannot be undone," said the pilot, rising to his feet and surveying the room. He looked very calm, and he smiled at the girls. For all their sorrow, they had to admit to themselves that the crown suited him very well; it shone as brightly on his pilot's cap as the circle of oaks in the forest of gold.

"Sire, sire," panted Bernard, letting go of the curtain and staggering toward Alberto. "This is all a terrible mistake. There's been a trick. There isn't any door! I've looked! There isn't any tree palace. It's nonsense. This boy was lying to you. You've handed your crown to a liar!"

Alberto blinked and shook his head. "A liar?"

"There *is* a tree palace," said the new king. "I've been there, several times."

The princesses stared at one another in confusion. *Several* times? But this pilot had only been with them for one night.

"I want to go there myself," announced Alberto. "If it *isn't* there, I'll take my crown back."

"Ah. It isn't possible to enter the tree palace simply because you want to," said the new king.

"You see! You see!" said Bernard. "Because it isn't there!"

"Not at all," said the new king. "You have to be a necessary guest, that's all."

Agnes looked with curiosity at the pilot. Had he been a necessary guest too? "It *is* there," she said, forgetting in her anger at Bernard that she was supposed to keep the tree palace secret. "You just have to know where to look."

"Yes," said Polina, drawing close to Agnes's side. "You saw the gold branch, Father. The silver leaf, the diamond."

Alberto looked from daughter to daughter in confusion. "I did," he said. "It's true."

Bernard scoffed. "He could have gotten those shining trinkets from any old market on his way here."

Alberto looked panicked. "That's true too."

"Sire," soothed Clarence. "Think of your retirement plans."

As if to settle the argument, the new king reached into his pockets to show a worn-out pair of shoes with holes in their soles. "If I have deceived you, sire," he said to Alberto, "it is over one thing only." He held the shoes out toward the old king. "Perhaps you will remember these?"

Alberto peered at the bashed-up shoes and turned pale. He started huffing and puffing. When Agnes saw the shoes for herself, and realized how the new king might have that particular pair in his possession, she gasped.

The new king dropped the worn-out shoes on the throne room floor.

He lifted off his crown, his pilot's cap and goggles, never once taking his eyes off Alberto. With a twist of his fingers, long locks of billowing hair fell to his shoulders, tumbling from their bindings—and Frida stood before them.

Frida, their brand-new king.

"I suppose you'd better call me Queen of Kalia, actually," Frida said to the stunned gathering as she twirled her pilot's goggles on her index finger, placing the crown back on her head with her free hand.

Bernard took one look at her and fainted to the floor.

"I knew it!" cried Agnes.

Alberto staggered away. *"Frida?"* he uttered. "But—"

"I *knew* you'd come back," said Agnes. Lorna fell to her knees in tears, and the other sisters laughed and whooped around the room.

"Queen Frida! Queen Frida!" Vita chanted.

"I promised, didn't I?" said Frida—expert pilot, new Queen of Kalia—as she opened her arms. Her sisters ran toward her, each of them hugging her tight, sobbing into her shoulders, kissing her face, patting her flying jacket, and trying on her goggles.

"Where have you *been*?" Agnes said. "How have you—"

"Didn't I say, Aggie? It's a big world out there," said Frida, smiling. "I'll tell you about it later."

"This is *impossible*," said Alberto, stamping his foot. "No daughter of mine knows how to fly a plane!"

"Oh, Father. This one does. It took me a few weeks, but I managed it."

"Frida, give me back my crown!"

"I'm afraid I won't be doing that, Father," said Frida firmly. "And as you once pointed out to me: with this crown, *I* am the law."

"But—"

"And Clarence is right. Thank you, Clarence. What about all those hobbies you wanted to take up in retirement?"

"But—!"

"You may keep the diamond as a token of my appreciation."

Alberto stared at his daughter the queen. The princesses watched with fascination as their father seemed to wrestle with himself without actually moving. His mouth bobbed open and closed like a confused fish's. His eyes boggled. He looked like a man having a tug-of-war with his own soul. And then he laughed—yes, Alberto, the man who had not laughed for months and months, began to shake, big belly hoots, wheezing squeals of what they dared to hope was joy. "Oh my, oh my!" he said.

"Are you quite well, sire?" said Clarence.

The old man stared at the adviser. "Quite well!" he said. "I think I may never have been better!" He opened his palm and looked at the diamond resting in the center, glinting and winking at him like a promise of a future he'd never dared admit. Then, to their astonishment, he ran from the room, tripping over the figure of Bernard, who was still lying in shock on the floor.

No one could stop the old king; he couldn't get out of there fast enough. They could hear the patter of his footsteps down the corridor, interspersed with occasional hoots and whoops, noises he hadn't made since he was a boy.

"Queen Frida," said Clarence, his thin face alight with pleasure as he emerged from the cluster of astonished staff. He knelt. "A great leader stands before us," he said. "It shall be an honor to serve you."

The other advisers looked at one another, wondering whether to follow Clarence's lead.

"A *queen*?" whispered one. "This is a bit . . . new."

"How glad I am I didn't call the new monarch a liar. Poor, stupid Bernard!" whispered another.

"But she isn't really new, is she?" said yet another. "Queen Frida is still the same brave, clever, thoughtful person she's always been."

"Indeed. And who knows Kalia better? No one."

They all fell to their knees before her.

"Thank you, Clarence. Thank you, gentlemen," said Frida. "But, please, get up. And stop whispering. We've got so much to do."

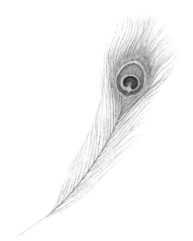

Eight
Peacocks and Paw Prints

Kalia was a very different place after Frida became queen. Bernard and a few others who weren't in agreement with a queen being in charge, particularly one so talented, were dismissed. Frida, aided by Clarence, filled her palace with people from all sorts of backgrounds and experiences. She became an excellent leader, and a great favorite among the Kalian citizens: fair, thoughtful, open-minded, and patient, not without a little bit of spark to get her through the difficult times. She can still be seen occasionally flying in her biplane over the city of Lago Puera, dipping and soaring over the famous Kalian sea.

139

About a month into her reign, she built a dance floor in the palace. It has black and white tiles on the floor, and multicolored lights that bob like fireflies, and every Friday all the people of Kalia are invited to come and dance. The food's pretty good too.

Alberto eventually recovered from his fit of giggles. He'd realized two things: firstly, that his daughter had been cleverer than him all along, and secondly, that his time as king was indeed over, and he could have some fun. Laughter seemed the best solution to these two realizations, and he packed his own suitcase and went off for a year or two of sightseeing. He took the diamond.

That was several years ago, in fact, and the princesses are still wondering if he'll ever come back. They each secretly, bafflingly, miss him. That's parents for you. The lioness was right: Alberto wasn't *bad*. No one's entirely bad, but they do get a little lost. And perhaps—just like his eldest daughter—in leaving, Alberto has found himself. He sends postcards from every country that he visits, and the palace fridge is covered with his missives.

Polina was appointed palace astronomer, and Delilah is head gardener; she still keeps a strong supply of dormidon, just in case, and advises the citizens on their herbs and vegetables.

Bellina is chief of foreign affairs, and since her appointment Kalia's wars with neighboring kingdoms have ended. Emelia is a vet and oversees the health of Kalia's livestock. Ariosta is a famous artist who shows her paintings around the world. Mariella keeps the kingdom's budget in order, and Chessa gives singing recitals and occasionally tours. When she's home in Lago Puera, the palace doors are open every afternoon for musicians to come and play. Lorna has established several schools for the people of the city, where lessons are available for all Kalian boys and girls. Vita runs a theater on the beach, and every summer the famous Kalian festival lasts for weeks on end. If you time your trip well, you can see some excellent plays. Flora is the palace librarian, and people flock from miles around to come and find a cosy nook, where they while away the hours with her excellent choice of books.

And Agnes? The one with the typewriter, who wanted to tell stories?

Let's just say I managed it.

As for the tree palace, you may well be wondering whether it really existed. People often do. The old king's adviser Bernard claimed it didn't, but that was only because he couldn't find it.

The truth is, we were so tired the night after Frida's coronation that we completely forgot to check if the door was still there. And with Frida crowned queen, and so many things for us to do, we never looked for that particular door again. We got older, became women of the world, our energies directed to the lives we had made. Yes, often, we thought about the tree palace, about Saleem and the lioness, and the toucan waiters, and the fun of dancing. But we were so busy upstairs that I must confess our thoughts about it lessened as the years went on. I think it is also true to say that none of us particularly wanted to revisit that windowless room where we'd been so unfairly cooped up for months on end.

That is, until yesterday, when a strange thing happened, and I had to write all this down.

Yesterday morning, a huge box was delivered to the palace door. I inquired as to who had delivered it, but the guard on duty had seen nobody. Neither was there any message. Except—next to the box, a feather had been laid, belonging to a peacock. And by its side, marked in the earth, was a paw print the size of a dinner plate. Gingerly, I opened the box. Inside was a pyramid of jam doughnuts.

142

I stood there, looking at the doughnuts—suddenly so familiar!—and my heart was thumping hard. I remembered the way Frida whirled and twirled under the multicolored lights, the way Ariosta swam across the lagoon, the way Emelia saved that little fox. It felt so long ago, and yet it could have been last week. Was someone watching me? I turned around, scanning the horizon—the Kalian sea, the shore, the green hills—but there was no one to be seen.

That afternoon, I took the box to Frida, who had just finished a meeting in the throne room with Clarence. The other princesses were all out of the city on various missions. Queen Frida's eyes lit up when she saw the doughnuts, and I told her how they'd appeared earlier in the day with no explanation, but for a peacock feather and a paw print.

Frida reached into the box and lifted one out. It was newly baked, and the sugar that dusted it glittered like tiny diamonds. "You don't think . . . ?" She trailed off.

I looked at her. "That's exactly what I think," I said.

She hesitated. "Do you know, Agnes, there are times when I might be brushing my teeth, or about to hold a meeting, or writing a letter—and I swear, I *swear*, I can hear a lioness's roar."

"Me too!"

"Oh, thank goodness. I thought I might be mad."

"It feels very far off, but strangely, I can feel it deep within me."

My sister the queen looked at me. Time had barely aged her, and she still wore exquisite shoes. "That's *exactly* how it is for me too," she said. "And I've been thinking about it, Aggie. I've no doubt that the tree palace is still there, that Saleem and the lioness and the toucan waiters and the jazz band are waiting for their next necessary guests. For although some things exist in places out of reach, that doesn't mean they cannot be."

(My sister really is a wise queen.)

"I always thought I'd never be able to go back. But shall we . . . shall we go and look tonight?" she went on, nibbling the doughnut. "Shall we go to that poky room and look behind Mother's portrait?"

I thought of Bernard the old adviser pushing aside the portrait of Queen Laurelia and finding nothing but a solid wall. I thought of the twelve of us when we were younger, finding the cold staircase and descending the five hundred and three steps to a world that gave us so much happiness. I was frightened to think of what we might find, but then I remembered the box of glittering doughnuts.

I must have been silent a long while, for Frida looked at me with concern. "Wise to pursue?" she asked me.

I smiled. "Wise to pursue," I replied, and we agreed on a time when the rest of the palace would be fast asleep.

And as I look at my clock, I see the hour has come. It's very dark and quiet outside in Kalia at this time of night; thanks to Bellina's international efforts, a peace has reigned for years. Frida's footsteps are coming up the corridor, and I see the golden glow of her lantern pooling. I can feel the old thrum of excitement in my heart. We'll walk the corridors of her palace together, my sister and I, hand in hand, the lioness's cry an echo in our ears. We'll find that old room and approach that portrait of our mother. We'll push it aside. And we will see.